DUE DATE

THE SPY LADY
AND
THE MUFFIN MAN

by the same author

THE NIGHT THEY STOLE
THE ALPHABET

THE SPY LADY
AND
THE MUFFIN MAN

Written and Illustrated by

Sesyle Joslin

Harcourt Brace Jovanovich, Inc.
New York

FOR Alexandra
with all my love

Contents

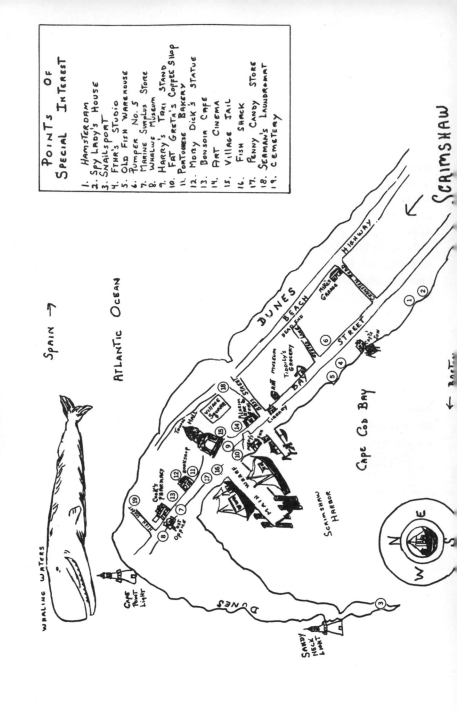

POINTS OF
SPECIAL INTEREST

1. HAMSTERDAM
2. SPY LADY'S HOUSE
3. SNAILSPORT
4. FTHR'S STUDIO
5. OLD FISH WAREHOUSE
6. PUMPER No. 5
7. MARINE SURPLUS STORE
8. WHALING MUSEUM STORE
9. HARRY'S TAXI STAND
10. FAT GRETA'S COFFEE SHOP
11. PORTUGESE BAKERY
12. MOBY DICK'S STATUE
13. BONSOIR CAFE
14. ART CINEMA
15. VILLAGE JAIL
16. FISH SHACK
17. PENNY CANDY STORE
18. SEAMAN'S LAUNDROMAT
19. CEMETERY

SCRIMSHAW

SPAIN →

ATLANTIC OCEAN

WHALING WATERS

DUNES BEACH HIGHWAY

MIKE'S GARAGE

STREET

BAY

ART MUSEUM

TIDDLY'S GROCERY

CAPE COD BAY

SCRIMSHAW HARBOR

CAPE POINT LIGHT

SANDY NECK LIGHT

DUNES

VILLAGE SQUARE

TOWN HALL

BOOKSHOP

COOK'S PANCAKES

POST OFFICE

MAIN WHARF

N E W S

Suggestions for Using This Log Book

In naval and merchant vessels the navigator usually makes an entry in the log-book every hour or half hour. In small yachts, however, this is neither necessary nor practicable. It will be found more convenient if entries are made and time noted when departure is made, when the course is changed, and when more important navigational aids are sighted or brought abeam.

If fairly long passages are made, it will be found useful however to make hourly, or at least semi-hourly, notations on wind, weather and barometer, since a concise review of this data is helpful in predicting weather changes.

In general, the completeness of the entries will be determined by the type and size of the boat, the waters she navigates, and the ambitiousness of the navigator. In sailing craft the sails carried should be noted in the remarks column.

Vessels spoken, incidents aboard, names of guests, etc., may also be noted in this column. Fuel and water, used and taken aboard, should be noted under proper headings since this information will prove helpful in determining the cruising range of the yacht.

Remember that the log-book is a legal document.

The responsible yachtsman will see to it that his records are concise and accurate for on his care and thoroughness depends the safety of his ship, his crew and his guests.

Date	Wind	Bar.	Ther.	Sea	Weather	Clds.
July 9	Calm	30	72	S.	B.	Cu.

TIME   REMARKS

2130   A strange black vessel has dropped anchor in the
        harbor. It sits in the moonlight like the ghost ship
        of an old sea-robber.

                                                    Eustacia

2240   Have checked position of unidentified ship from
        widow's walk. *It's anchored direct. opposite us.*
            What if they're the Smugglers still mad about
        last summer and back for Revenge?
            And the Reward Money too?! Advise all mem-
        bers of S.S.F.T.D.A.S.O.C. to sleep with weapons
        under pillow.

                                                    Squid

Date	Wind	Bar.	Ther.	Sea	Weather	Clds.
July 10	Mod. gale	28	68	R.	F.	S.

TIME	REMARKS

0630   Last night's ship pulled up anchor and is heading out to sea. Looks like just an old trawler this morning.
       Although maybe that's just its disguise.

       Arab

0900   Spied a *body*. About several hundred yds. down the beach, lying half under small dock near Capt's Inn. Looks pretty dead from here. Investigating immed.

0920   Am back. It was only a smelly old sand shark washed up on shore. Worse luck.

       Squid

1405   *Village Patrol Report*

       Me and Parvis cased wharf. Found suspicious fellow with checked cap sneaking off the Boston steamer. Tailed him down wharf far as Charley's Hot Dogs, but then had to run for cover as Fthr. suddenly loomed around the corner. Pretty sure he didn't recognize me, though, because of beard.

       Arab

1700   The fog covers us like a soft gray mouse. There is a big wind that's been howling and blowing around all day. I wonder does it have some place warm and cozy to go when finally it's out of breath and little again?

Rachel

1730 What the wind does in between times is its own business and not the S.S.F.T.D.A.S.O.C.'s. And from now on all Log entries have got to be more factual and made out professionally, can't you?

Squid

2200 At about 2130 heard banging on my bedroom shutter. Thought it was the wind, so naturally did not bother to answer. Banging got louder, and then this *pssssting* came through shutter. Somebody was out there on the roof! Quickly turned off light, hid Log Book and pistachio nuts under bed. Just in time. Shutter kicked open, letting in sheaf of rain and a small dark stranger in brown cape and black bowler. He had a terrible big bulbous nose, small sinister eyes, and looked altogether like a toadstool. The poisonous kind. Just then door burst open and Squid rushed in, switching on the lights.

"Would you *mind* taking off my nose?" he snarled at the stranger who quickly obliged and who I now saw was none other than the Arab.

"Who said you could take my new nose without even asking," Squid screamed, "and you wore it out in the *rain*."

"It didn't shrink or anything, Ham, honest," the Arab mumbled.

"Hah!" Squid said, and taking out a handkerchief, he delicately wiped his nose and put it in

13

his pocket. "Hah!" he said again, curling his lip in that nasty way he has when he can't think of anything sarcastic enough to say, and he slammed off.

I felt sorry for the Arab looking so wet and downcast and gave him what was left of the pistachio nuts to take to bed.

I can't think why Squid wants to be such a pig with his nose.

Eustacia

Because it cost nearly a month's allowance and it's the only decent one I've got.

Squid

Date	Wind	Bar.	Ther.	Sea	Weather	Clds.
July 11	C.	30	70	C.	M.	N.

TIME	REMARKS
0930	Tide is coming in and I see somebody's foot afloat I think. It is a terrible slime green. (Gangrene?)

I went to look and it wasn't a foot. It's a boot. Well, I guess I was pretty close. I fished it out with Oma's clam rake, poor thing. I think some people must be very cruel and heartless to just go and throw a boot away like that. Especially into the ocean and alone without even its mate. How do they think it must feel?!

Contessa

Voice from floor pipe: S.S.F.T.D.A.S.O.C.?

Squid: Maybe. Who's calling?

The Arab: Me, the Arab.

Squid: Anyone with you?

The Arab: Yes. Parvis.

Squid: State position.

The Arab: Under deck. Rear drainpipe. Do you read me? It's urgent! Over.

Squid: Line's clear. Over.

The Arab: Well, I was going off duty because it's getting dark out and nobody's around anymore, and then all of a sudden I heard these two men come dragging something down the beach. And one of them says: "Maybe we ought to just bury him here." And the other one, he says: "Yeah. The sooner we get rid of him the better. I never knew they started in smelling so fast."

Squid: Good work, Arab. I'll be right there.

2010   False alarm. Turned out to be just these two fellows trying to get rid of a big old tuna head. Squid got really mad, but I don't see how I was supposed to know they weren't murderers. He got so mad, Squid did, that he ripped off my moustache and flung it into the bay. I think he'll be sorry, though, because salt water in quantity isn't at all good for moustaches. Unless they are made from human hair, and even then if you're not careful they can get all curled up around the edges.

Arab

The green-eyed lighthouse blinked an answer to the distant foghorn. Nothing else stirred in the night except for us who had gath. quietly into Squid's room for a meeting.

First we checked over the equipment and found some of the disguises need fixing up, like the curls have got uncorked from the blonde wig. Also sev. magnifying glasses are clouded up with salt air. Then Squid discovered we were almost out of fingerprint powder, which was a mystery until the Contessa confessed to using some after her bath. This made Squid angry, partic. as he doesn't believe in baths. Then we got down to business which didn't take long as there isn't any.

"We've only got two dollars and eleven cents in the Mutual Fund, but four of them are Canadian," said the Treasurer.

"And not even a Case in sight," the Arab complained. "Last summer by now we were already after the Smugglers."

"We've just got to be patient," Squid said. "Wait long enough and something bad's bound to happen."

Just then we heard footsteps creaking up the stairs.

"Who's that?" the Contessa whispered.

There was a pause at the landing, and then the footsteps started coming heavily down the hall.

"Quick," said Squid. "Hide everything."

The steps stopped, fumbling, at the door, and then through the keyhole came this familiar and disgusting sound which is something between a belch and a hiccough.

"It's Parvis!" cried the Arab, and we all breathed again with relief.

"Drunk as a billy goat, I bet," said Squid. "Better let him in."

The Contessa pulled open the door, and Parvis, with his hair all in his eyes and smiling in a very silly way, staggered into the room.

"What'd I tell you?" Squid said. "He's three sheets to the wind."

"Oh, Parvis!" cried the Contessa in a sad, reproachful voice. But he just grinned like an idiot and lurched across the room, tracking in sand and an awful smell, as he tried to kiss everybody hello.

"Pugh!" cried the Arab. "You stink, Parvis! What've you got into this time?"

Squid gave a professional sniff. "Fish manure."

"Oh, Parvis," cried the Contessa, throwing her arms around him, which is a v.g. example of her unselfish kind of love. "Why do you have to drink?"

"He's got no willpower, that's why," said Squid.

Poor Parvis looked round at us puzzled; then he stopped grinning and hung his head.

"It's no good going on at him when he's already drunk," I said. "Anyway, it's not his fault the way everybody uptown's always giving him a drink."

"If he could only learn to refuse," the Contessa said.

"Can't teach an old dog new tricks," said the Arab, and after that the meeting broke up.

Date	Wind	Bar.	Ther.	Sea	Weather	Clds.
July 12	Light breeze	29	71	C.	M.	N.

TIME   REMARKS

1030   Will have to go on hard rations t'day since it's so squally in the kitchen. All that happened was I lowered the pulley from top deck into kitch. window, same as always, only when I gave the Arab the hoist-away signal, instead of the provision sack, up came Oma's skirt. I guess the hook got stuck into her by mistake. She was pretty upset. She said it was because we made her ruin the clam chowder, but I think she just didn't want anybody to see she wore such long underpants even in the summer. I said we wouldn't tell.

                                                              Squid

1530   Build two (2) fires fifteen (15) paces apart.

                 Put two (2) great tubs of water to boil. Cut up the whale into easy pieces. Flense pieces and put the blubber into boiling water.

                 Allow to boil until all blubber is rendered into oil.

                                                                Arab

1610   What the devil is *that* supposed to be?

                                                                Squid

1700   It's a recipe for making blubber oil, stupid, what'd you think? I don't see why we can't do something practical while we sit around waiting for a Case. I bet the Strawberry Man would help us peddle it.

Arab

1730   Jared Samuel, you are a cruel and horrible person. How can you talk like that about some poor whale who's never hurt you and has probably got a wife and children somewheres?

Rachel

ALL LOG ENTRIES HAVE GOT TO STICK TO FACTS AND ALIASES, DAMNIT.

Squid

Date	Wind	Bar.	Ther.	Sea	Weather	Clds.
July 13	Mod.	28	66	C.	F.	S.

TIME   REMARKS

1430   *Special Report*

All members of the S.S.F.T.D.A.S.O.C. on Red Alert. Suspect there's going to be trouble brewing in Scrimshaw.

At 1300 the Arab and me were at the Wharf keeping watch on Arrivals and Departures. Nobody special came in or left except for this whopping 500-pound tuna on the *Annabel*.

Then along comes the Beach-Dune Taxi Ride back from going over the dunes, and all the tourists get down and then out climbs this v. mys-

19

terious person. To begin with, she's wearing a black trench coat and likewise a big black hat slouched over her face, and it wasn't even raining!

But the big question is how come she was getting *out* of the Beach-Dune Taxi Ride when she hadn't ever got *in* in the first place? Least of all not in the village like the other passengers because we were right there when it took off. *There is only one deduction to make from all this: If the Beach-Dune Taxi Ride picked her up out on the dunes, how'd she have got out there anyway unless she's some kind of spy whose submarine dropped her off. Or even space ship,* like the Arab said. Well, so then she pays the Dune-Taxi in a deep foreign accent, just like you'd expect, picks up a black briefcase(!?), and walks across the street to Harry's Taxi stand.

"Please take me to number 620 Bay Street," she says in a low voice, and gets quickly inside.

The Arab gave me a poke, his eyes practically popping out of his head.

"Hey," he said, "620! That's next door to *us!*"

Exactly.

Squid

1715   Kept watch on next door from widow's walk. Caught glimpses of new suspect prowling through the house, going in and out of all the rooms, upstairs and downstairs, as though she were searching for something. Then she went out on sun deck and I got a good look with field glasses. She is v. pretty in an exotic, foreign way.

Her face, set on graceful neck, is like a long-stemmed flower of the night, with petal-pale skin and large dark eyes, perfect for hiding secrets in.

She was still wearing the trench coat and stood by the rail smoking a cigarette in a long holder as she gazed out over the bay, a dark and mysterious figure. I wouldn't be surprised if Squid and the Arab are right about her. I mean she certainly looks like a spy lady all right.

Eustacia

2345   It is almost midnight, but suspect has still got a light on upstairs. Maybe it's a signal to the craft that dropped her here. It's really not so surprising, either. I mean a spy coming here, because when you think about it, a little fishing village like Scrimshaw, right at the edge of the ocean and everything, could be a very practical place for espionage. It's just a lucky thing she landed next door to us, that's all.

Arab

Date	Wind	Bar.	Ther.	Sea	Weather	Clds.
July 14	Gent. breeze	30	72	C.	M.	N.

TIME   REMARKS

0830   The Spy Lady's at work already! Spotted her from top deck at 0809 when tide was at peak low. She was way out on the flats, surveying the harbor and taking pictures and everything!

Squid

1145   Was keeping watch on next door from widow's walk with Fthr's binoculars and caught sight of Spy Lady through living room window v. carefully putting her black briefcase on top of desk. She dusted the top with handker. but never opened it. Squid said naturally not as it is probably fitted out with explosives for emergency action, like 007's briefcase.

                                           Eustacia

1645   Mike's Garage just left this car out in front of the Spy Lady's. It is a big old dark blue Bentley with a suitcase in the back seat and long Swiss license plates, but they may just be fakes. The Arab overheard the mechanic telling Oma, who was hanging out the wash, about how it had been towed in from the Beach Highway where it had got stuck near the dunes. Well, that's *her* story.

                                           Squid

1900   I have finally just seen the Spy Lady for my own self! I was on the top deck with my spyglasses, and she came out on her bedroom balcony in a *emerald dressing-gown trimmed with white fur.* She has a long stream of raven hair, and she brang a silver hairbrush with her. She stood with a sad smile at the sea. Then it suddenly thundered and lightninged and she went quickly back in.

      I think she's the most beautiful person I've ever seen even if she is a Spy Lady.

Maiden Fair

"Summer lightning
very frightening," said a maiden fair.
"But I must not weep,
Just try to sleep," she said,
brushing back her hair.

By
Rachel

2100   Damnit, *Contessa,* are you trying to wreck the
Log Book or what?

And what'd you expect anyway? Spy ladies
have to be beautiful. It's part of the job—stupid!
And I've already warned you a hundred times if
you can't memorize your own false name, you're
not going to belong anymore.

Squid

2200   Ugh. You really make me sick and tired, Hamilton Samuel, with your damned bullying. Rach's
only a child after all, and if you don't quit pick-
ing on her, I'm going to tell what happened to
Fthr's cigars. And I *don't* care.

Persis

2230   What happened to them, Squid?

Arab

2300   None of your blasted G. damn beeswax.

Squid

Well, how do you think your poor Father would feel if he was to know the way you kids carry on with all your awful swearing like a bunch of drunken sailors, as if he don't have enough to worry about as it is, poor chap. And don't think I don't know about them cigars neither.

Your friend,
Mrs. Beverly Cook

A New Beginning

The four persons, sun-red as a clump of beach plums after a day at the Herring Run with their Father, returned home in the bay-dusk, and retiring directly upstairs, we very nearly fainted dead away with surprise and horror to find Mrs. Cook sprawled there in the Log Book. If we had got found out so easily by the twice-a-week cleaning woman, what chance would we have with a professional Spy Lady?

We went straight away into the Contessa's room since it is the best for secret meetings as it is full of stuffed animals who Squid says absorb the sound. Also it has only one window to black out, which we did with the rug. Parvis was then elected to guard outside, and we quickly got down to the terrible business at hand.

"From now on," said Squid, "we have got to be prepared to guard the Log Book with our lives. Any suggestions?"

There naturally were, and the first thing we did was to go back to the printed directions in the front of the Log and circle in red where it says, "Remember that the log-book is a legal document." Now we shall have a constant reminder of how v. careful we have got to be.

Squid thought we should draw the circle with our blood mixed together so that it would also serve as a solemn oath of brotherhood, but as we are already that in any case, I said I thought it would be a pretty silly waste of good blood.

"You're just afraid of blood, that's all," said Squid.

"I am not. But there are things I like better. Ink, for instance."

The Arab looked up from polishing his magnifying glass.

"You can wash out blood stains quicker than ink," he said, which I had to admit could be an advantage.

In the end we circled the sentence with the Contessa's red crayon and after that made the following impt. decisions:

(1) Only one person from now on will keep the Log Book, and since I am the oldest and already Secretary of the S.S.F.T.D.A.S.O.C. anyway, that person is to be me.

(2) The Log Book when not in use must remain at all times in its new secret hiding place. Where this is was the Arab's idea and very clever of him, too, although more than that I cannot say.

(3) Hereafter Log Book entries will not be so concerned with the weather and will stick to Remarks.

(4) Never again shall swearing be written down on paper where it can be held as proof against you. Henceforth all swearing out loud will simply be let blown out to sea to join the chants and curses of the ancient mariners.

After drawing up this new set of rules we then got to the main event on the agenda, to wit: the Spy Lady.

The Arab sat there looking v. thoughtful. "I bet she's going to turn out to be a lot harder to solve than last summer's Smugglers."

"Naturally," said Squid. "Spy ladies are a much harder nut to crack. That's why they use them."

"What's our plan of operation?" I asked.

"Simple," replied Squid. "Keep her under constant surveillance until we find out what she's up to. Then draw the net in."

We were here interrupted by a foghorn which kept blasting off very close by until finally we realized it was coming from the kitchen and must be Oma blowing for supper, which is what she does sometimes when she is feeling salty. The meeting thus ended and we slipped quietly out of the Contessa's room, except for Squid who tripped over Parvis.

"!" Squid cried, clutching his foot in pain, although I don't really see how a person could stub his toe on anybody as soft in the head as Parvis.

The next morning I had first patrol and was on the widow's walk at 0700. True, I wasn't altogether awake yet, but then, neither was the rest of the bay. The sea gulls swooped around with lazy calls while beneath them the sandbars seemed to stretch sleepily out to touch the incoming tide, and the sandpipers hurried, hurried to find their breakfast.

I watched over at the Spy Lady's for a long while, but nothing even stirred. The house just sat there, strangely still and unblinking in the early sun. Later, at breakfast, we found out why, and it was a terrible shock.

Ham, Jared, Rach, and I were already at the dining room table when Father wandered in.

"Hello!" he said in that startled way he sometimes has when he comes across us unexpectedly or early in the morning. I believe it is not so much our size as number that surprises him. Jared says that absentmindedness is a common trait of the artist. I haven't noticed it in him, Jared, yet, and he is already a v.g. artist himself, but perhaps it is because he is too young and hasn't enough left over to forget about.

"Would there by any lucky chance be a blueberry muffin left?" Father inquired. He is v. fond of them, poor man, and I am sorry to confess that usually there aren't because we are such hogs. This morning, however, due to some oversight, there was one, and Fthr. was very surprised and happy.

"Thank you, my dear fellow," he said jovially to Parvis who brought him his newspaper. "Well, well," he added, taking a closer look. "I am glad to see you looking so clear-eyed and sober. And what a nice cold nose you have, too."

Here the breakfast table began to rock as Parvis is shamelessly grateful for any kind of compliment and kept jumping up to shake Fthr's hand.

The reason I am recording all this is to show how normal everything was and how without any warning the following blow fell.

"Well, what do you think of it?" Oma called out from the kitchen. "She is gone already."

"Who is?" asked Rachel.

"The pretty lady next door," replied Oma.

"Yes, so she is," Fthr. said, but as he was inside his newspaper by now, it was impossible to tell whether he meant yes, pretty, or yes, gone.

Squid meanwhile had put down his spoon and turned v. pale.

"Gone?" he said hoarsely. "How do you mean gone?"

Oma passed a pitcher of milk through the hatchway and gave him a look. "What do you mean how do I mean? She left. How else can you go?"

We looked at each other, our spirits going down so fast you'd think they had lead sinkers; then miraculously they were caught up by Oma's next words.

"She likes it so much here in Scrimshaw, that's why she's gone. To arrange for her things to get shipped down. That, anyhow, is what Mrs. Cook has heard. First she rents the cottage for one week only; now she decides to take it for the rest of the summer. I suppose she wants a nice little hideaway to rest and relax," Oma ended up, which shows how unsuspecting and innocent people who are grown up and then some can be.

Squid signaled us with his eyebrows, and we quickly excused ourselves from the table as who could eat after news like that anyway?

The Contessa sighed. "I hope she isn't going to stay away for long."

"So do I," Squid said grimly.

The Arab's forehead creased up with a worried frown. "You think she's really going to come back?"

"Well," Squid said, "it sort of figures, doesn't it? She must have come just to case the place first. I mean we even saw her doing that, and then when everything works out to specifications, she decides this is the right place for the job and goes back to get her equipment and everything."

Although Squid's deductions were pretty reassuring, we

still hurried next door to investigate and see if we could pick up any further clues. The Spy Lady, however, was every bit as careful as you would expect, and except for a map (?!) on the coffee table in the living room we found no telltale signs that she was coming back or had even been there for that matter. Until, that is, we got around to the bathroom window, where at last we discovered a key piece of evidence: to wit, the Spy Lady's toothbrush.

"There, she's left her toothbrush! That proves she's coming back," cried the Contessa who has v. good teeth-cleaning habits.

"It might only prove she doesn't care," said the Arab who has not. Even he, however, admitted it was probably a good sign, and we felt so cheered that we went straight up to the village and bought two new disguises and another magnifying glass so as to be ready for the return of the Spy Lady.

We also decided that as the Log Book has already got this new beginning, we might just as well get on with it as best we can while we wait for the Spy Lady's next move.

Father always says that when you are creating a picture, you get a better perspective if you fill in the background of a canvas right away, which we did not, of course, but better late than never.

I thought first that I would describe us all, a page each. Then I thought on and realized that everybody had much better write his own description. They won't be as accurate that way, but on the other hand nobody will get mad at me.

Jared said that he would draw accompanying portraits of us.

As well as myself, I will have to do Fthr. and Oma since they don't even know they're here to begin with.

The Opposite of a
Rogues' Gallery and Various
Confidential Information

RACHEL ALIAS THE CONTESS

Rachel Giulia Samuel

Right now I am 42 ¾ in. high and 10 in. across. I just measured to make sure. I am 8 years old and have sort of blue eyes and sunburnt hair. My most favorite ice cream is pistachio.

When I grow up I might go to Africa and be a Veterinarian. I would also like to be an Actress. And a Ballet Dancer. In between times I will have lots of little children and write poems and stories like Persis does. I think it is silly to be only one kind of person.

Also when I am grown up I am going to keep a Home for all stray things like my broken-off comb and this piece of pencil. Certain people say why do you feel sorry for a thing that doesn't have any feelings? But I don't see how they can prove that a thing doesn't have feelings like everybody else.

JARED Alias THE ARAB

Jared Bernard Samuel

Name: Jared B. Samuel
Age: 9⅔
Kind: Male
Height: 4 ft. 2 in.
Weight: 61 pounds
Hair: Brown
Eyes: Blue
Birthplace: Boston
Business Interests: Whaling
Other Affiliations: S.S.F.T.D.A.S.O.C.
Marital Status: Single

HAMILTON ALIAS SQUID

Hamilton Samuel

I am 138 months old, have blazing red eyes that spin and spark off like pinwheels when I am angry, ears like conch shells, long chestnut curls, and stand 7 feet tall without my shoes. My favorite dessert is molten iron, and I think it would be pretty idiotic for the founder and President of the Secret Society For The Detection And Solution Of Crime to go around writing out descriptions of himself.

PERSIS ALIAS EUSTACIA

Persis Samuel

I am twelve and one-half years old but tall for my age, like Father. I have light brown hair and greenish blue eyes. We all of us do, more or less. In the summer I also have freckles. Oma says they will go away with lemon juice, but they never do. They must have a different kind of lemon where she comes from. Or a different kind of freckle.

My favorite pastimes are reading and writing, and I mean to be an author as soon as I am old enough.

I was born April the 4th under the sign of Aries who is a ram. Chives, onion, radish, hops, peppers, and wormwood all belong to my sign, which doesn't sound like much of a bouquet to me.

Aries people have the following characteristics: will, the urge to act, the spirit of enterprise, leadership, impatience, and rashness. Which now that I've got it all written down actually sounds much more like Ham than me.

PARVIS

Parvis Samuel

I just realized that I would have to do Parvis's page as well. The trouble with having a dog who is practically a human being is that sometimes you forget he isn't.

Parvis is a tall and handsome Afghan Hound with beautiful long hair the color of molasses. He is nine years old, but the way dogs figure that makes him even older than Fthr. although he doesn't look it.

Parvis is clever, brave, and an excell. protector. In fact, sometimes you can hardly go swimming without him trying to save your life. Another of his outstanding traits is being an exceptionally keen judge of character. He is better than a lie detector as he can tell with one sniff whether a person is criminal or the opposite.

Parvis is also faithful, gentle, and loving. I can remember when Rachel was a baby he used to rock her cradle and push her carriage and sometimes even hold her bottle. As a matter of fact, for quite a long time Rachel used to think Parvis was her grandmother. I don't know why exactly except that she was a pretty smart baby in a queer sort of way and probably got the whole idea backwards looking at Little Red Riding Hood.

Although Parvis is usually the casual ambling sort, he can also be v. athletic and move like the wind. In fact, it was really due to his being so fast on his feet that we caught the

Smugglers last summer, even though he was a little drunk at the time and may have thought he was back in his homeland chasing gazelles.

Which brings me to Parvis's one bad habit: drinking alcoholic beverages. I guess it all began because of how he is so friendly and likes to ramble around the village visiting with the fishermen and everybody. In a way I suppose he looked like just another long-haired artist, and so one day somebody treated him to a beer, and that's the way it started. Mostly he only drinks on the weekend, and you can always tell even before he gets home by watching him come down Bay Street with a sort of rolling walk, like a sailor navigating a deck on a high sea.

Parvis has taken more room than I would have thought. I am near the end of his second page, so I will finish by stating that he is our greatest helpmate and favorite companion.

Jonathan Samuel

Father is Jonathan Samuel, and Jonathan Samuel is a sculptor. He has a whole big loft studio up the street next to the old fish warehouse. It is covered with signs like No Trespassing, *Verböten,* Beware of Live Wires, *Pericoloso.* But they are only meant to keep us out, not the customers.

Fthr. is a portrait sculptor, but he also sculpts a lot of other things more abstract than people's heads and which I cannot describe as I do not always know what they are even when I am looking at them.

When Fthr. makes a sale, we are rich for a while although never for long because of spending so much money celebrating being rich again. In between times we try to cheer Father up and remind him of all the artists who became famous after their time.

Father is tall and I think weighs a medium amount. He

has deep blue eyes and brown hair with a widow's peak just like Jared's. When he starts work on a new sculpture, he is even more absentminded than usual and goes around with a sort of glazed stare which makes him look a little like a stuffed hawk. The rest of the time he is v. handsome. He is also loving, kind, understanding, and has a very good sense of humor.

Oma

Oma means grandmother in German, and although she isn't really our grandmother, she is certainly as good as.

I am beginning to see that although you can choose to be a writer, you cannot always choose what you write. So I will quickly put down that Oma has taken care of us ever since our Mother died. It has been a very long time now, but we still miss her badly sometimes, even Rachel who was not much more than a baby and hardly knew her. I would never have supposed that somebody's empty place could be just as much there as a filled one. More even, because a minus seems so much bigger, the way it goes off into nothing.

Oma comes from Austria and looks so plump and fresh and crisp you might think she has stepped out of her own oven.

Aside from being kind, affectionate, and a v.g. cook, she knows some unusual things like how to whittle whistles and how to manage a cockfight. She has also taught us how to hand-wrestle the way it is done in the Tyrol. We almost never win, though, as she is as solid as an oak. Which reminds me of something else about Oma, and that is no matter what's happened she is always the same looking and acting. In one way it is tiresome, but then in another way it is very comforting. I think she must be like one of those wooden Russian dolls and that inside her you would just go on finding a whole lot more Omas, one inside the other, getting smaller and smaller.

Now that we are all lined up so neatly, I suppose I might as well go on and put us in our house and the house in the village. Perhaps by that time the Spy Lady will have come back.

Hamsterdam is a big lopsided house and pitches right over the bay. When the tide is out it sits up on shore like a landlocked ship, and when the tide comes in at night it gently rocks the whole house to sleep. This is where we live in the summer, and we are always v. relieved to find it is still here because it is so old and tottering you would think one more storm would wash it out to sea altogether. It is covered with weather-gray shingles and has a widow's walk on top that makes you think of misty whaling ships and brawling buccaneers. In fact, it did once belong to an old whaling captain named Elizah Laughton, which is how we came to find this Log Book in the first place as well as some old journals and ship's ledgers.

Each person has got his own room, and they are all odd shapes and queer corners with some floors that slant so much you can slide down them. The outside of the house is nearly as good as the inside. Besides the widow's walk there are two sun decks, upper and lower with good secret quarters under the latter, amongst the underpilings. There are also great expanses of roof with dormer peaks and an excell. skylight which spies right down over the bathtub in the bathroom below.

Scrimshaw is a little fishing village at the tip of Cape Cod. On one side is the bay and harbor lined with old wooden cottages all stacked together like playing-card houses. Off on the other side are the sand dunes, and if you walk over them, it is like crossing a high rolling desert until finally you come out at the Atlantic Ocean.

Half a mile straight up Bay Street is the center of the village where the wharves and the shops and the sidewalk artists are, and it is usually awash with tourists. There is a special summer smell here of sizzling hot dogs and onions and hot chocolate fudge and fresh Portuguese bread and, of course, fish. All the deep-sea fishing trip boats dock at the main wharf and so do the real fishing vessels like the *Mamma Lucia* and *Little Joe,* and so for that matter does the Boston steamer.

One of the best days in the summer is the Blessing of the Fleet Day when the Bishop comes over from Boston to bless the boats and pray for a good catch. All the fishermen scrub up their trawlers and paint them fresh and polish the brass and put up colored nets and flags for decoration. Even the dinghies get all decked out and parade around the harbor as proud as a bunch of four-masted schooners. That night there is a Fishermen's Ball at which Poseidon and his wife Amphitrite are Guests of Honor. At the stroke of midnight, they spring upon their winged horse and gallop down the wharf from whence they dive back through the vasty green to their palace below, where they live happily ever after on clam juice and sea muffins.

"Hey, what do you think you're doing?" Ham demanded, reading the Log Book over my shoulder. "That's none of it true facts, that last part!"

"Can I see?" said Rachel, coming over from the doll's cradle where she had been rocking her clam to sleep.

"What's a sea muffin?" she asked.

"It's made out of minced seaweed and chopped-up clam," I said without thinking.

"Oh, Persis!" Rachel gasped, racing back to her clam's side. "How can you! You'll hurt its feelings!"

47

You have to be careful what you say sometimes as Rachel is such a loyal person and can get pretty unhappy if she thinks a friend is being discriminated against. Actually her clam is quite nice as clams go, and I didn't mean to upset either one of them. Rachel found it the first day we got here. She calls it honey clam and carries it around with her most of the time, which is all right with the rest of us as it is usually nice and quiet. At night the honey clam sleeps in a glass of water on her bedside table although Oma says it is dangerous as Rachel might wake up thirsty and drink it by mistake.

I suppose now that the honey clam has got in here, I better include the others who live with us not hitherto listed, and maybe Jared will do their portraits as well. First there is a sweet young sea gull named Icarus. When we found him, we thought there was something wrong with his wings, but it turned out he just doesn't like to fly. Fthr. thinks heights make him dizzy, and, in fact, he does get quite a giddy look whenever he's up on the roof with us. And least but not last, Jared has a red anthill. Then there is James who is a very well-groomed and intelligent hamster. Hamilton has taught James to carry messages and whistle although not, of course, at the same time.

"What's that?" Squid suddenly whispered.

"What's what?" I asked, hardly looking up from my Log writing.

"Sshh!" cautioned the Arab as Squid moved swiftly to the shutter window and opened it, letting in the black night.

The Contessa put the honey clam in her pajama pocket. "Who's out there, Squid?" she asked in a wavery voice.

Even as she spoke we saw a light go on in the house next door.

"It's her!" Squid whispered hoarsely. "The Spy Lady's back!" He stepped away from the window, pale with excitement. "Quick, put out the light," he

JAMES

ICARUS

RED ANTS

The Return of the Spy Lady

said.

Several days have gone by between the beginning and the end of that sentence, which cert. makes it the longest one I've ever written. It was not by design, though, as once the Spy Lady was back, there were many things which needed putting into the Log Book. The problem was the Log Book itself. By some awful mischance it had got firmly nailed into its secret hiding place by Johnny Four-Fingers, the handy man who comes around to fix things up after storms. Four-Fingers is not, of course, his real name, but it's what he's called in the village because that is all the fingers he has got left on one hand, which only goes to prove how little he can be trusted around the house.

I will not recount all the trials and tribulations we had getting the Log Book free again, but will simply state that finally we did it and it is safely up here on the roof with me right now where I plan to record all the missing entries whilst the Contessa and I are keeping watch on the Spy Lady's house. Since this is to be a long vigil, the Arab has hoisted us up some supplies: e.g., 2 hunks of Portuguese bread, 8 garden tomatoes, and some bacon (cooked).

We have also got Icarus the gull with us for protective coloring. That was Squid's idea in case the Spy Lady should chance to look over here, but I don't really see how anybody could mistake us for a group of sea gulls. Least of all Icarus himself, the way he cowers on the roof and sits so carefully back from the edge with his feathers ruffled up around his neck like old Queen Elizabeth.

But all this is now, and Squid said not to go jumbling things up as we shall need the facts of the case in their proper order, so I will go back to the Spy Lady's return.

It was a desolate and foggy night with neither stars nor moon. We stood in the shadow of my room and watched the Spy Lady's lamplit window gleaming like a question mark in the dark, and the Contessa's teeth set up a loud clattering.

"Ninny," said the Arab.

"I'm not," she chattered.

"Then hold onto your teeth, can't you," Squid hissed, and covered her up with his sweater although I believe what was in the atmosphere was less cold than chilling. Everything was so still it seemed that even the air was too frightened to move in the dark. Then a gull flew by following its own lost cry, and the next moment the Spy Lady appeared in her window.

"There she is," gasped the Contessa.

"Look at her," said the Arab. "She's got ostrich feathers on her bathrobe."

"Camouflage," Squid grunted.

The Contessa sighed. "She looks like a picture, doesn't she?"

And it was true, she did, although not an ordinary Scrimshaw one, the way she stood framed in the window, lone and mysterious in her continental robe and long dark hair.

"A spy picture, maybe," the Arab said.

Just then she raised her head, and although we stood in the dark, it seemed that she was looking right up at us.

"Duck, everybody," Squid whispered, and we all dropped to the floor, from whence after a safe interval we crawled off to our beds.

The next morning I was awakened by somebody walking across the foot of my bed. Fortunately, it turned out to be only James the hamster carrying a neatly folded message between his teeth. Bundled in his fur coat, eyes alert, he traveled over the peaks and valleys of the bedclothes like a stout little Bavarian agent rushing across the Alps. In exchange for a piece of apple, he let go the note, but as Squid had taken the precaution of writing in lemon juice, it took some time over a candle to burn out the following message:

Laiceps C.O.S.A.D.T.F.S.S. gniteem ta
tsafkaerb. Llet eht srehto.

I did, and we all hurried downstairs to breakfast although in the end we didn't have the meeting until afterwards as Oma's face kept rising in the hatchway like the
morning sun.

"Zoh," she said, beaming. "I hear the next door lady
came back dead in the night."

The Contessa gasped and Squid dropped his knife.

"She means in the dead of night," the Arab said.

"I know what I mean, thank you."

"Come on," Squid muttered from a far corner of his
mouth. "We better split up and meet outside."

"Right," said the Arab, snatching up a couple of blueberry muffins.

"Turkeys maybe gobble, but other people should at least
try to eat like ladies and gentlemen," Oma said. "And leave
some blueberry muffins for your Father."

But it was too late, for they were already gone and so by
then were we.

Squid blew his bos'n's whistle, and the meeting convened
under the bottom deck. As the tide was beginning to come
in, we were obliged to settle ourselves along some of the
higher shelves and corners of the underpilings.

Following appear the Secretary of the S.S.F.T.D.A.S.-
O.C.'s notes in their original form.

The Contessa: I feel like a monkey up here.
The Arab: You look like one, too.
President: Order! Order!
The Contessa: Well, so do you.
Eustacia: "I went to the animal fair
                   the birds and the beasts were there—
                   the big baboon

        by the light of the moon
        was combing his auburn hair.
        The monkey he—"
Squid: SHUT UP.
The Arab: Hear! Hear!
Squid: I have called this special meeting of the Secret So-
        ciety For The Detection And Solution of Crime so that
        we can discuss the methods and procedures for the Spy
        Lady.

Upon this opening remark the members of the S.S.F.T.-
D.A.S.O.C. straightened up on their shelves and focused
upon the President their now sober and alert attention. He
continued as below.

Squid: For instance, what actual facts have we got on her
        so far?
Eustacia: None.
Squid: Exactly.
The Arab: Told you she was a slippery character.
Eustacia: I wonder if we'll get as big a Reward for her as
        the Smugglers?
Squid: Well she wouldn't be much of a Spy if there wasn't
        a good price on her head.

This exchange of financial matters reminded the President to ask for the Treasurer's report.

Treasurer: The Mutual Fund is now empty and owes
        $1.40, that sum having been loaned to us by the kind-
        ness of Mr. Jonathan Samuel. Our father.
The Arab: We know who he is, idiot.
The Contessa: I'm not an idiot.
Squid: Order, blast it! (pause) Thank you. (pause) Well,

the Treasurer's report confirms that we certainly need some Reward Money all right.

The Arab: We could buy some new fingerprinting equipment.

Squid: What we really need is a lie detector set.

Eustacia: And some new disguises.

The Arab: Yes, what I want is a nose of my own like Squid's only a nice big hooked one.

The Contessa: I think we ought to keep some of the money for emergencies.

Squid: She's right. Then the next time we get poor, we can give it to Father.

Eustacia: I hope he won't be too proud to accept.

The Contessa: We could just leave it under his pillow.

Eustacia: Anonymously.

The Arab: Well, that takes care of spending the Reward. Now all we got to do is figure out how to get it.

Squid: Elementary, my dear Arab. Find out what the Spy Lady's master plan is and outwit her.

Eustacia: We better start recording all her comings and goings.

Squid: And chart all her movements around the area.

The Arab: And watch to see if any other foreign agent tries to contact her.

Squid: Intercept any messages she receives.

The Contessa: But what if she turns out to be a good Spy Lady?

Squid: Don't worry. She can't be all good.

The meeting was then quickly adjourned as Parvis came dashing in under the deck to get us. He was in a v. excited state and kept going around in little yipping circles until he was sure we were following him, and then he took off down the beach, his long hair flying out on all sides of him.

"He's certainly on the track of something," the Arab said, and indeed he was, for he led us directly to the breakwater wall on the other side of the Spy Lady's house, where we arrived just in time to see Mr. Silva the Moving Man unloading his truck.

"It's all her things come," said the Contessa.

"Clever boy, Parvis," Squid said, but although this was his favorite compliment, Parvis paid it no heed. He just started in jumping up and down v. agitatedly, and then we saw why.

"Look, it's her," whispered the Arab, and there was the Spy Lady standing in her doorway, watching as Mr. Silva came staggering up the walk under a great pile of baggage and boxes, etc.

"Hoop-la," she said as he nearly tripped. "Careful, please. Careful!"

"They're probably packed with explosives," Squid whispered.

"This way, Mr. Silva." Her voice was deep and flavored with a French accent, and, in fact, a writer might have gone on to compare it to some kind of delicious dark chocolate dessert if she didn't already know it belonged to a dangerous foreign agent.

Meanwhile, Parvis was giving soundless little yelps and his tail was whirling like a bearded propeller. It was clear he meant to take off after the Spy Lady, for as previously explained he is an uncanny judge of character and can tell the bad from the good a mile away.

"Restrain him," Squid ordered. "We want to keep her in one piece."

The Arab tackled Parvis just as he was about to leap over the breakwater, and the rest of us fell on him as he is quite large and difficult to keep down when excited. For safety's sake, we stayed sitting on him as we watched Mr. Silva carry in the following items:

Two pieces of matching velvet brocade luggage in the shape of olden carpetbags. They were so stuffed they were bulging, the Arab thought probably with foreign currencies.

Four potted plants, flowering and otherwise. The largest had an exotic purple bloom to it, and I thought it the prettiest but agreed with the others that it was no doubt poisonous.

A portable typewriter, or at least that's what it looked like from the outside.

One topless carton which seemed to be full of nothing but writing pads, notebooks, paper, pencils, and erasers. Squid was not surprised, saying that if you just considered the secret messages alone, you'd realize how much paper work a Spy Lady has to do.

A short-wave transmitter cleverly disguised to look like a portable hair-dryer.

Mr. Silva then unloaded two final and startling items which I do not mind admitting filled us with dread. The first was a violin case which did not, of course, fool us for a moment.

"It's how they always carry submachine guns," Squid said, although the Arab argued in favor of a jeweled dagger set which he said was more her type.

The second item was a huge dark green trunk which Mr. Silva lightly and cheerfully carried in one hand.

"It's empty," whispered Squid, and we four looked at each other in astonishment.

"An empty trunk," said the Arab. "Very convenient."

The Contessa stirred uneasily. "What's the Spy Lady want an empty trunk for?"

But nobody answered as the rest of us had been struck dumb by some very sinister possibilities.

"Maybe she collects seashells," the Contessa said, although even she looked rather uncertain.

The sun had slipped away behind a great gray cloud, and we suddenly felt cold sitting there.

"Nor'easter brewing," the Arab said, and we decided to postpone further investigation until the following morning. We then got up off Parvis, who had meanwhile fallen asleep, and went home.

Operations the next day began later than usual as at breakfast Fthr. was looking round for volunteers to do some chores and naturally found us.

By the time we had finished swabbing the decks and washing the sea spray off the windows, Rachel forgot where she put the honey clam, and so we had to make up a searching party as she was getting pretty upset. Hamilton finally found the clam tucked in the toe of her sneaker, gone unnoticed as it had formerly been Jared's and was a full size too large. The shoe, that is, not the clam.

We finally got to our post on the widow's walk and from here found a good view of the Spy Lady. She was sitting on her sun deck, draped in a sort of sari, as yellow, thin, and summery as a butterfly's wings, and was writing in a large notebook although we couldn't tell what as even with the binoculars up to full power we were too far away to read over her shoulder. I said was writing, but the fact is we could see she was also erasing. In fact, she seemed to be erasing as much as she wrote, if not more.

"Pretty cautious, all right," said Squid, almost admiringly.

"What do you suppose she's putting in there?" I said.

"It could be the key to the whole mystery," said the Arab.

"What *is* the mystery anyway?" the Contessa asked.

"Use your head, stupid," Squid said. "If you knew, it wouldn't be a mystery, would it?"

After a while the Spy Lady got up and went into the

house, leaving her notebook alone on the chair. That was her first mistake as the Arab was quickly assigned to go and get a closer look at it, and that, of course, was ours.

While we covered him from the widow's walk, the Arab dashed across the way intending to shinny up the bulwark post in front of the Spy Lady's sun deck from whence he could see the notebook. But the post, alas, was still wet and slippery from the last tide, and the Arab slipped down as fast as he shinnied up. Squid finally began to get worried about the time and signaled him to return, but the Arab stayed where he was, answering back with semaphore signals, only as he didn't have the flags and was also hopping around with excitement and/or nervousness, it was very difficult to read his message. Nor, we now saw to our dismay, were we the only ones trying, for the Spy Lady had come back out and, unbeknownst to the Arab, was at the deck rail looking down at him. Now any other observer might have thought the Arab was only fooling around, doing calisthenics or something, but we knew that she of all people would recognize his secret signals for exactly what they were: secret signals. We sighed with relief therefore when she turned away and went into the house, but we needn't have bothered, for a second later she was back with the very violin case which contained her submachine gun or set of daggers. Our hearts' blood froze as we saw her calmly unlatch the case, and with screams and cries of warning to the Arab, we threw ourselves down flat on the widow's walk.

The Arab fled to safety behind some old breakwater rocks, but by then we were witnessing something far more surprising than an armed assault, for what the Spy Lady withdrew from her violin case turned out to be a violin.

"She's a violin player!" cried the Contessa happily as the Spy Lady did, in fact, begin to tune up.

"And a lot more devious than I even suspected," Squid muttered darkly.

*   *   *

How true this was we experienced more fully about a week later when for the first time we came face to face with the Spy Lady—or at least the Contessa did. The morning had started out pretty much the same as the others, for like all well-trained agents the Spy Lady seemed to go on schedule. So far every day she worked in the notebook (?!), played her violin which Squid says must be some kind of smoke screen, and lately had been observed going up toward the village around noon. At circa 1130 on this partic. day, we four were fully disguised and well hidden under an old abandoned dinghy full of peepholes near the Spy Lady's house when her telephone rang. This was, of course, just what we'd been lying in wait for, and when she went inside to answer it, we hurried to her living room window. She spoke in a low voice but clear enough for me to copy down into the field notebook.

"Allo? Ah, yes. I am glad you have checked with me. Today we have a little change from the usual. Listen carefully: 4 rolls, 1 red cheese, six eggs—"

The Contessa nudged me. "What're *you* writing down her grocery list for?" she whispered.

"That's her code, idiot," Squid said, quickly shushing her up.

"—3 lemons, and a beefsteak. That is all," the Spy Lady concluded hurriedly.

We fled back to safety under the dinghy, and the episode would have ended right there had not the Contessa dropped her clam in our flight for cover.

"Oh, my poor little honey clam!" she cried, and before any of us could stop her, she ran right back into the face of danger: to wit, the Spy Lady's. For the latter had not only come back out but down onto the beach and now stood watching as the Contessa, oblivious to our frantic signals of danger as well as the danger herself, went on plowing and sifting her way through the sand until at last she triumphantly plucked up her honey clam at the very foot of the Spy Lady.

"Ah, so it was a lost *clam* and now you have found him. Marvelous," congratulated the Spy Lady as though some of her best friends were lost clams.

The Contessa squealed like a frightened pig when she looked up and saw who it was she was sitting at the bottom of.

"And what is your name?" inquired the Spy Lady in a v. casual way.

Squid, the Arab, and I cringed behind the dinghy, but although the Contessa rolled her eyes nervously, she managed to hold onto her tongue.

"Perhaps then," the Spy Lady suggested, "you are but a sea nymph and like your friend the clam also without voice?"

Here I must insert a description of the Spy Lady's smile which accompanied the above remark as even from where we were, you could see what an outstanding characteristic it was. My experience with smiles has been that most grown-ups only have time enough to do it with one part of their face, while the rest goes on with whatever it was doing in the first place.

The Spy Lady, however, took her own good time about the whole thing. Her smile began and rose and spread until her entire face was lit up like a sunburst. It was so disarming it was practically sinister. Another example, as Squid later said, of the many ways a Spy Lady has to catch a person unawares, and the poor Contessa was no match for it. She blinked and faltered and, tugging shyly at her wig, smiled back.

"Ah," said the Spy Lady, taking quick advantage of her gain, "but surely someone with so nice a smile also has a name?"

"The Contessa," confessed the Contessa with still another smile, as Squid swore under his breath.

"I see, and which Contessa would that be?" the Spy Lady wheedled. But the Contessa at last caught sight of our signals and, thinking quickly, gave a great shrug and let loose a volley of her favorite gibberish talk. She is actually quite good at it and can make it sound almost like Italian, which she likes doing to remind people that she was the only one of us to be born in Italy. This is not because she is Italian, however, but because of all the good marble that Fthr. went there to sculpt with, like Michelangelo. Then Rachel got born and after a while we all came back home.

The Spy Lady looked a little startled by the Contessa's foreign outburst, but before anything else could happen, the latter had taken heel and run off.

Squid was furious with the Contessa, of course, and all the way through lunch kept threatening to demote her although, as the Arab pointed out, there wasn't anywhere lower she could go, except maybe underground.

"Of all the dumb, stupid, idiotic things to do I ever heard of, running out from cover right into the open like that."

"I know. I know," cried the poor Contessa. "And I wouldn't have—it was only I had to go after my clam."

"He's always getting lost! Of all the dumb, stupid animals, can't you put him on a leash or something?" Squid roared. "Then going and telling your name! And it wasn't even like you were being threatened or tortured or anything."

The Contessa's chin started to quiver.

"Don't be a baby," the Arab said.

"I'm not," the Contessa mumbled, shoving chunks of bread into her mouth to dam up the tears.

"Anyway," I pointed out, "it wasn't her name she told. It was only her alias."

"Only!" Squid choked, but you could see even he was beginning to feel sorry for the Contessa as he said no more and even let her finish his dessert.

That afternoon the Spy Lady was observed to be casting more than one eye in our direction, and Squid said we ought to proceed with caution as everybody knew discretion was the better part of valor. I said if that was the case, wouldn't the best part be not to proceed at all? In the end we voted to lay low for at least twenty-four hours, which was a mistake as the minute Oma saw us sticking around in the house, she made us clean all the junk out of our closets. Except, of course, for Rachel who never will and flung herself on the floor of her closet like Joan of Arc defending the fields of France, as the more old and broken a thing is the less she'll throw it away because the sorrier she feels for it.

The only business that got done during this time was the Arab constructed an intercom system out of some chicken soup cans (empty) and Fthr's new fishing tackle, which fortunately the latter didn't mind as he has just begun this summer's new big work and is too absentminded to have noticed. Also Squid composed the following pledge of allegiance for the S.S.F.T.D.A.S.O.C. and sent copies around with James so that everybody could memorize it, esp. the Contessa.

> Eyes to the front, Eyes to the rear
>> Ears to the wall.
> Hark to the cry, Hark to the mo-an
>> Trusting of no one
>> Suspicious of all.

After this interval one more event took place which I must record, and then the Log Book will be all the way up to date. This occurrence was unbelievable even to we who witnessed it, and featured Parvis.

It came about when the Arab, on top-deck watch, spotted the Spy Lady's black trench coat and hat going up Bay Street head-strong into the blustery rain. We quickly pulled tufts from an old feather Icarus wasn't using anymore to see which of us would shadow her. It turned out to be Squid, me, and Parvis, so we three stuck on our disguises and slipped up the street after her. Keeping the black coat carefully sighted, we tailed her all the way into the village to the Pilgrim Bar and Grill. While she went inside, we stationed ourselves across the street behind a stack of lobster traps next to Perry's Fresh Fish and waited.

It occurred to us afterwards that something wasn't altogether right by the way Parvis acted. Or didn't, for far from having to be restrained from lunging after the Spy Lady as before, all Parvis wanted to do now was fool around with a bunch of lobsters. But that is hindsight, which is so useless a thing I wonder why anybody ever bothered to give it a proper name. What happened at the time was we just hid there until the Spy Lady emerged, and when she did, it was a terrible surprise, for from the front we saw it wasn't the Spy Lady at all we had been tailing but just another black coat.

Squid's face fell. "How'd that happen?!"

"It must have been all the fog." But this did not comfort him, no more did the Old-Fashioned Penny Candy Store, even though I treated which ought to have, considering how expensive an old-fashioned penny candy can be.

By the time we were halfway home the weather if not our spirits had lifted, and then even they did, for as we went past Pumper No. 5 Parvis gave this kind of strangled yelp. He stopped cold, his nose pointing across the street, and I very nearly yelped myself, for there coming around the corner of Fthr's studio was the real Spy Lady. Before we even had time to wonder what she was prowling around there for,

Parvis wrenched himself free from Squid's clasp and, quivering with that pure instinct which leads him to recognize the villains from the others, charged across the street at her. Squid and I sank behind a rosebush in some fright, issuing commands, calls, and whistles, all of which Parvis ignored. It was a terrible moment, but just as I was going to shut my eyes so as not to see the bloody attack, Parvis leapt into the Spy Lady's arms and covered her with kisses.

"He's gone crazy," Squid gasped.

The Spy Lady was meanwhile petting Parvis right back.

"Bonjour, mon petit lapin," she said, referring I guess to his disguise, an old rubbery pink rabbit mask which fortunately he had managed to keep on.

Squid blew masterfully on his bos'n's whistle, but Parvis just went on kissing the Spy Lady and even shook hands with her. Finally she gave him a last pat and went off up Bay Street while he stood politely watching after her, his tail still wagging.

"I don't believe it," Squid whispered hoarsely. "He's gone out of his mind." He whistled again, and with a last look after the Spy Lady, Parvis ambled back across the street to us. He had such a self-satisfied air you'd have thought he had just single-handedly captured an entire international spy ring instead of the other way around.

"Maybe he's drunk," Squid said hopefully. I sniffed at him through the rabbit hole, but he only smelled like onions which Oma always makes him eat if she thinks he's coming down with worms.

"There's got to be some explanation," Squid said, pulling off his nose and moustache with a worried gesture. We trudged toward home in a baffled silence until Squid stopped and snapped his fingers excitedly.

"I've got it!" he cried, his eyes lighting up. "What it is, see, is the Spy Lady's obviously wearing some kind of supersonic perfume! You know, like an ultra-high frequency whistle that'll only attract dogs!"

I congratulated Squid heartily on his keen thinking as it wasn't until much later, in fact this very moment, that it occurred to me to wonder why should the Spy Lady want only to attract dogs?

From Hamsterdam

to Snailsport

SQA002 (49) (29) LB044
L SUA274 PE NL PDF NEW YORK NEW YORK
MADELEINE SOPHIE LEHMAN DASH CHOTTLEY

The above telegram was delivered to the Spy Lady by Harry's Taxi Service at about 1830 today. This is the first actual piece of evidence we have in the Case of the Spy Lady, and as soon as we have ironed out all the wrinkles in the paper, we're going to put an Exhibit A label on it.

This morn. had started out like all the others with nothing to warn us that it wd. turn into such a red-letter day. At 0930 the Spy Lady was spotted settling down on the sun deck with her notebook. From 1030 on she was several times observed to be checking on the time, the tide, and the sun.

"Whatever she's plotting," the Arab said, "I'll wager it's something really big."

Squid gave him a sharp look. "Are you referring to inter-planetary espionage?" he asked in a low voice.

"I could be," replied the Arab thoughtfully. "One good look, if we could just only get one good look into that note-book."

Squid started cracking his knuckles. They went off one by one like a handful of Chinese firecrackers. Knuckle-cracking is probably Squid's worst character trait, but as it usually precedes a good idea, I suppose it is worth it. In this case the idea was to rig up a mirror on the small dock oppo-site the Spy Lady's sun deck, thereby catching a reflection of her notebook which the Contessa, who is v.g. at mirror writ-ing, would quickly read. It was, I think, quite a good scheme and might even have worked if it hadn't been such a gusty day. As it was, however, the mirror blew down almost at once and broke into at least seven years of bad luck, which as far as I can see started right then.

To begin with, the Spy Lady soon gave us the slip and got away unobserved in her Bentley. When her trail was next picked up, she was swimming way out where the tide was beginning to come in although how she managed to get into the bay undetected I do not know. The first we heard of it was the excited three clicks-three clacks three clicks from Oma's teeth (false) which the Contessa was signaling with as our old Morse key had broken down.

"Look out there!" she cried as we gathered around her on the upper deck. "Way out by the nets! I just saw this big peppermint-striped fish!"

Squid swiftly adjusted his telescope, surveyed the horizon, and then turned around with a loud groan. "What kind of nut are you anyway? I ought to take away your lookout duty, I really ought to. Peppermint fish!" he said. "It's the Spy Lady, you idiot!"

It was, too, but in all fairness I think it ought to be recorded that this matter of mistaken identities, i.e., Spy Lady versus peppermint fish, was not entirely Rach's fault since due to her spyglass having got lost, she was sighting through an empty paper towel roll.

"Look at her go," said the Arab. "She's swimming underwater the whole time"

"What'd you expect her to do, walk?" Squid grunted.

"She's coming up!" cried the Contessa, and up indeed came the Spy Lady's neck, long and curved and glistening like a swan's in the sun. The rest of her followed suit, and she got all the way out of the water and climbed up on the breakwater rocks.

It was now clear why the Contessa had mistaken her for a peppermint-striped fish; to wit, she was enclothed down to the knees in what looked like a red-and-white striped old-fashioned bathing costume although was no doubt a bikini in disguise.

The Spy Lady stretched out flat as though to sunbathe, but considering all the barnacles on the rocks, it was unlikely anybody would lie there unless they had to, and so, as the Arab sugg., her plan was probably to signal a prearranged airplane with her stripes. Something must have gone off schedule, though, as the only plane that finally came flying low over her was the Scrimshaw Sightseeing Service, after which she came ashore and went into her house. We did likewise as Oma was blasting for lunch, which on Tuesdays means clam chowder. It also means trouble although it never used to in the old days when the Contessa loved clams in a more platonic way like the rest of us, such as: fried or chowdered.

There is not enough time, however, to go all the way into the clam chowder which, as it happened, nobody was able to do in real life either owing to the Contessa who dressed herself and the honey clam in black mourning and sat throughout the meal eyeing us in silent reproach.

In any case it is better that I get back to the telegram as when Squid last inspected the Log, he said the entries kept on jumping all over the place like Mexican Jumping Beans. It is all right with me if that is what he wants to say, but I think I ought to point out that it is not v. accurate as I once had a pair of Mexican Jumping Beans for a pet(s) and they never did anything more than twitch.

By 1700 that afternoon it had turned misty and blowy, and we four were in the house. I was tidying up the Log Book, mainly trying to get out all the eraser crumbs. Hamilton was off taking care of James. Jared was walking around the living room on his knees and flapping his arms encouragingly at Icarus. He is always trying to teach him to fly by some such means or another. As for Rachel, she had her nose stuck in a book, which proved to be a v. messy affair as it was made from some of Fthr's putty and not yet dry.

"Where's Ham?" she now asked.

"He said he was going to get James curried for dinner."

Rachel gasped and turned a sickly color.

"Curry as you do with horses, not rice, stupid," Jared explained, and Rachel's looks improved, especially as Hamilton and James then entered the room, the latter chirping away between his bulging cheeks.

"Don't talk with your mouth full," admonished Hamilton, a pretty useless piece of advice to pass on to a hamster as when isn't it?

No further conversation was recorded as we sat half lulled by the sound of the wind and the rising tide slapping up against the house.

"Sssh!" Squid suddenly cautioned, and listening through the sea sounds, we heard a car stopping next door and a door slam.

Squid hurried to look out the window. "It's Harry's Taxi," he said, and darted quickly out on the front porch. He was back the next moment, his cheeks flushed.

"What's up, Squid?" the Arab asked.

Squid carefully shut the door and came slowly and thoughtfully over to us.

"Harry brought down a telegram," he said. "The Spy Lady's got a telegram."

"That's funny," said the Contessa, "so does Parvis!" and in truth the latter had at that same instant come bounding into the house with a telegram which he dropped at Squid's feet. From the name and address printed thereon, T. Symond, 620 Bay Street, we quickly surmised that the Spy Lady's telegram and Parvis's were, in fact, one and the same.

"Well done!" cried the Arab. "How'd he manage to pull that off?"

"Good boy, Parvis!" said Squid. "What must've happened," he mused, pacing up and down the room as he reconstructed the scene, "she must've tore open the telegram, memorized it instantly, see, like they're trained to do, then tried to get rid of the evidence, naturally, which is where good old Parvis came in!"

The latter, hearing his name pronounced so richly, stopped his crazy prancing and stood tall and proud, his long aristocratic nose held high, like a French general waiting to be kissed on both cheeks and decorated in the middle.

"Dear clever Parvis," cried the Contessa. Parvis tossed the hair out of his eyes and grinned. Clearly even he had begun to believe himself the best telegram retriever around, whereas the truth is Parvis will retrieve anything just as long as it's been thrown away first. Which can be quite an annoying accomplishment when it happens to be something like an apple core that you hadn't been planning on seeing again so soon. This, of course, is why Oma gets so flustered whenever any company comes with suitcases, and starts in mumbling about how there's never even a cabbage leaf unstuffed in this house let alone anybody's drawers. Referring, of course, to Rachel on the one hand never throwing anything away and Parvis on the other bringing everything back.

"There!" Squid hissed triumphantly over my shoulder as he, the Arab, and the Contessa clustered uninvited around my chair. "That's just exactly what I mean about Mexican Jumping Beans in the Log Book!"

"Can I see?" said the Contessa.

"Why don't you just get on with the telegram?" inquired the Arab.

Well, as nobody had a clean white handkerchief, we picked up the telegram with a pair of pincers the Arab had invented from the claw of a lobster (dead) and removed it to the sun room. We chose this room as it hangs over the bay and commands a perfect view of the harbor and in partic. the back of the Spy Lady's house. It also has a big round oak table which is very convenient when there are four persons examining evidence at the same time.

Squid placed the telegram directly below the light, and a row of sharp little marks now became apparent.

"Careful," he warned. "It might be injected with something fatal."

"What do you mean?" cried the Contessa, quickly dropping her corner of the telegram.

"You've heard of poison-pen letters, haven't you? So why not a poison-pen telegram? It'd be even faster."

The Arab polished his magnifying glass and bore down on the telegram. "I'll wager these are actually some kind of toothmarks."

"If that's the case," said Squid sadly, "they are probably only Parvis's."

We then set about studying the contents of the telegram which, as it is by now some pages ago, I might as well reproduce again.

```
SQA002 (49) (29) LB044
L SUA274 PE NL PDF NEW YORK NEW YORK
MADELEINE SOPHIE LEHMAN DASH CHOTTLEY
```

"I think they forgot to put in the message," said the Contessa.

"Idiot," Squid said. "That *is* the message."

"Which, then, top or bottom?"

And well may she have asked as the one looked as indecipherable as the other.

"Bottom, stupid. Those digits and all are always up top. They're the telegraph people's code—"

"I wonder what Western Union's got to hide?" the Arab mused.

"—and what's left of the telegram," Squid cont'd., "is the Spy Lady's."

"Made/leine So/phie Leh/man Dash/ Chott/ley," murmured the Contessa. "It sounds like the start of a nursery rhyme."

"Only to somebody still in the nursery," said the Arab.

"I am not," the Contessa began, but was interrupted by Squid, consulting his cipher chart.

"We can try it this way—say, if Made is the key word, then M might equal Y, but in that case A would only equal A and D would be G—so that's no good."

"It still looks to me," the Contessa said, "like a lot of people signed it and forgot what they were going to say."

"What makes you think they're people just because they have names?" inquired the Arab.

"That's right," said Squid. "They could be a convoy of ships or some rockets that the Spy Lady's supposed to go meet."

"Or blow up," said the Arab.

"But what about the DASH?" I asked.

"Elementary, my dear Eustacia," replied the Arab. "It's like they always say STOP in telegrams, only the opposite."

"Wrong," said Squid. "In this case it could only be the kind of DASH you use in somebody's brains out."

"Well, I don't think so," said the Contessa. "I think it's one of those fancy Lady So and So dashes whose name gets called out in ballrooms by red-velvet footmen."

"There she goes again!" cried Squid. We thought, of course, he was referring to the Contessa's flight of fancy but, following his gaze out the window, saw he actually meant the Spy Lady who stood on her sun deck in a yellow slicker windbreaker, her hair blowing to all points, as she made ready to jump into the sailboat moored below.

"We're right so far then," said the Arab. "She's got some kind of rendezvous at sea.

"It's getting rough," said the Contessa. "I hope she's careful."

"Don't worry," said Squid, pulling on his boat sneakers. "We can't afford to lose her yet."

"There she goes," reported the Arab, at the window. "She's leaving vicinity of Hamsterdam and appears to be heading in a northeasterly wind out toward Snailsport, riding a choppy sea at I would judge about 15 knots."

"Come on," cried Squid, already half out the door. "Everybody on board!"

I must quickly explain here that Snailsport is the end of the peninsula which curves round the bay and lies opposite us, although it won't be found on any navigation maps or fishing charts, no more than Scrimshaw, as they all appear in the Log under their code names.

"Eustacia!" Squid screamed from below deck. "Come on, blast you! Hurry up or she'll get—"

It is now tomorrow, and after yesterday's tragedy our spirits are so low and heavy you'd think there was an old sea-rusted anchor tied to the other end. I don't even feel like finishing up Ham's preceding bellow but shall anyway as I do not want to be accused of leaving old pieces of sentences lying around the Log Book.

"—lost in the fog."

As it turned out, that is just what happened anyway although, to be more accurate, it was not so much the Spy Lady as we four who got lost.

Sea tailing is hard enough even under good conditions, but as well as bad weather, we had a late start. This was due to a last-minute pocket inspection of the Arab and the Contessa since you cannot be too careful about checking overweight when you are sailing a beloved but elderly craft like the *Landlubber*. In addition to the usual S.S.F.T.D.A.S.O.C. equipment, for instance, the following Marine Surplus Store items were found on the Arab's person:

> 2 whale's teeth
> 1 lobster pot buoy
> 1 set of ball-bearing wheels
> 3 Haitian tree snails

1 can of parachute
4 large square corks

He was quickly relieved of all but the corks since, as he pointed out, we might need them to help keep us afloat, which shows the kind of optimistic way the Arab thinks even when he is being pessimistic.

The Contessa carried a much lighter load than usual: the honey clam, half a bag of red-hot devils, and a one-eyed piece of driftwood.

"OK for the honey clam and the red-hot devils," said Squid, "and No for the driftwood."

"But it's for good luck," said the Contesssa, and was swiftly admitted aboard, for as all hands know a little luck can carry you a long way, and that is just what happened although not at all in the sense it was meant.

The fog was moving in and we could no longer see the Spy Lady's boat but:

"Man the sails!" cried Squid, and off we went, caught up by the wind with the salt spray blowing hard on our faces.

"Thar she blows!" Squid called from the prow, and the Arab, who is always hoping to come across a whale, nearly capsized us although it was, of course, the Spy Lady to whom Squid referred.

"Quick, to starboard!" he commanded, and for a brief moment somewhere between the gloaming and the mist we sighted the Spy Lady's sail.

"I see her!" cried the Contessa, sounding so pleased you'd have thought we'd caught sight of a Lorelei on a Rhine rock instead of a Spy Lady on the brink of espionage although, as we were now about to find out, all we had actually caught was a red herring.

"Hold her to port," Squid shouted through the wind, but at the same moment the Spy Lady changed course and her boat, in view for only another instant, headed back to shore.

"I guess she didn't know it was going to be so choppy out here," said the Contessa.

"Come about!" Squid shouted to the Arab. "Head for Hamsterdam! Turn back, idiot!"

"All right," yelled the Arab, "if you're so smart, then where's back?!"

With these words we now saw clearly, or as clearly as was possible, that we were not only caught up in a near gale but wrapped in a fog as thick as cotton wool.

"Hold on, everybody!" cried Ham, himself grabbing a tight hold on Rachel, and huddled together, we bumped along in that pocket of fog like a bunch of young kangaroos in their mother's pouch, only probably a lot more worried.

"I wonder if that's Oma calling us for supper," Rachel said wistfully as a foghorn blasted several times from the other side of the mist.

"If it's anybody calling us for supper out here, it's probably Davy Jones," I replied, although not out loud as I didn't want to scare anybody, least of all myself.

You'd have thought it was nothing more than a beach stone the way the runaway *Landlubber* went skimming and skipping across the bay. We held on for dear life and wished for nothing more in the world than to stop. Only then when we did, we wished we hadn't, of course, for the *Landlubber* hit upon a shoal and with a last quiver leapt half out of the water like a harpooned fish. Which is just what we were. Harpooned, I mean, for a rock had pierced right through the *Landlubber*'s underside, and we watched, horrified, as the sea went gushing in and out like our own life's blood.

"Well, anyway," said Squid, "at least we're still on the same continent."

This was true. The fog was beginning to lift and we could now see where we were, which was not the coast of Spain as we had begun to fear nor even Boston, but the tip of Snailsport. Yet as known to us in the sunshine as our own backyard, so in the deepening twilight did Snailsport look unfamiliar: a long strange pale arm that stretched into the sea and had gathered to its ghostly reefs how many old rumrunners before us?

"All hands on deck or what's left of it," Squid said, sounding a lot more cheerful than he looked.

We hauled the poor old *Landlubber* up on shore as far as we could go, which happened to be next to the half-buried hull shell of an ancient schooner.

"I hope there aren't any old pirates out tonight," the Contessa remarked, with a nervous look around.

"Don't be silly," I said. "They're all dead."

"That's what I mean," she replied.

Squid now called an emergency meeting of the S.S.F.T.D.A.S.O.C. to discuss the Ways and Means of Survival. It proved to be discouragingly short, as follows:

President: What is the Transportation report?

Transport. Comm.: One wrecked-up sailboat plus six feet, but they won't do us any good until maybe after midnight when it's low enough tide to get back to the mainland over the village breakwater.

President: How come we're missing two feet?

Transport. Comm.: Well, if it's that late, I figure you-know-who will be asleep and we'll have to carry her.

Food Comm.: I will not!

President: The Food Committee will kindly keep her remarks to business.

Food Comm.: We've got ten red-hot devils which four people don't go into, but if we cut them in half, the candy, I mean, then we'll have twenty which is more even.

Transport. Comm.: I knew I should have got those cornflake survival bars. They had a whole barrelful up at Marine Surplus.

Food Comm.:   I think I'd have rathered survive on chocolate bars.

President: Does the Communication Committee have a
   report on smoke bombs or torpedo flares?

Communication Comm.:   That's a stupid question. How
   can I when we've never even been allowed to buy any?

President: It's just as well. I mean if we called attention to
   ourselves, the wrong people might get to us first.

Food Comm.:   I thought you said you didn't believe in
   ghosts.

President: I was referring to the Spy Lady, imbecile!

The meeting was then adjourned, and the four of us sat
down on a log to wait to be rescued and tried to keep each
other's spirits up, although it is true we often sank them by
mistake.

"All I got to say," Squid said, "is if the Spy Lady had all
this figured out, she's a lot cleverer even than I thought."

The Arab glanced over his shoulder at the dark dunes
waiting behind us.

"You think they might be planning an ambush?" he whispered.

"I just hope they're alive, that's all," said the Contessa,
with a shudder.

We began to worry now about Father getting worried.
Then Ham said what if it was one of his very absentminded
days and he didn't even notice? So then we worried about
that instead because even though we knew Oma would remind him he used to have four children, what if anything
had happened to her?

Rachel clutched the honey clam close to her. "It's getting
dark," she said in a small voice, and as the darkness grew
larger, so did her voice get smaller until finally both the day
and Rachel went out altogether.

"If I'd known we were going to be shipwrecked," Jared

said, shivering next to me, "I'd have bought some of that old Navy underwear. It was insulated and everything for only 69¢."

"That's because it was just the top part, stupid," said Ham.

"So what's stupid about keeping your top warm?"

This naturally led us into a debate over which section would you choose to keep warm, top or bottom, but even this conversation soon died out as voices in the dark, even the ones you think you know, can begin to sound v. strange.

The weather had meanwhile cleared, and we could see the stars and a moon stilettoed above, while across the calmed water all the bay houses blinked like a long string of festival lights. I think it must have been quite a pretty sight although, to tell the truth, between some of us watching out for an ambush and some for phantoms, we didn't exactly have the time to appreciate it.

I don't know how much longer we sat on in the dark like that, expecting the worst, but soon enough we were startled by the sound of a motorboat in the distance and a ghostly voice ahoying above it.

"What's that?" whispered the Arab.

"Sssh!" Squid hissed.

The Contessa's head, which had dropped off to sleep in my lap, now stirred. "I know what it is. It's a ghost."

"How could it be? Ghosts don't have motors."

"Maybe not the really old ones, but what about the others?"

The motorboat drew closer, and in it we dimly made out a tall sepulchral figure standing between the sea and the sky.

"Ham-Persis-Jared-Rachel!" it called.

"He knows our names!" cried the Contessa, throwing herself back into my lap.

"Sssh!" Squid warned, and holding our breath, we sat as

still as four bumps on a log while the boat headed in to shore.

"Rachel, Persis! Where are you? Ham? Jared! Ahoy, boys, are you there?"

This time the voice was close enough to sound v. familiar.

"It's Father!" I cried, jumping up.

"No wonder he knows our names!" said the Arab, and we raced down splashing pell-mell into the water to greet the boat and flung ourselves over him. It was a very happy re-union as all of us were feeling esp. grateful that Father was our father, except, all things considered, maybe poor Fthr. himself. He was much too nice, though, seeing our general condition (poor) to make any comments until we were wrapped up in blankets and headed back for Hamsterdam. Even then he only said not to worry about the *Landlubber,* which would be as good as old once it got patched up, and that he trusted in the future we'd have a lot better sense than to go out for a sail in that kind of weather.

"Oh, but we didn't just go out for a sail."

"We'd never have done it if we hadn't to have."

"That's right. It was business took us out."

"We hadn't any choice. Once the Spy Lady left next door, we had to follow her," yet another voice blundered out. To our surprise this voice turned out to be mine, proving that you cannot trust the most careful person not to talk. What was worse, it also proved that you cannot trust the most absentminded person not to hear, for of all our voices going off simultaneously it was mine that Fthr. heard.

"The Spy Lady next door?! The Spy Lady!" Father repeated, astonished. "Surely you don't mean Madame Symond?"

"Madame Symond?" we in turn repeated, astonished, for we had no idea that Fthr. even knew her name, or alias as it no doubt was.

"Oh, no," Father groaned. "Not again. Not last summer's

smugglers all over again." He took a deep breath. "Well, this time I'm sure you're on the wrong track. Madame Symond," Father cont., stumbling over her name despite he is v.g. at French, "from what I have observed seems to be a perfectly ordinary, harmless, and charming lady. And I want you to promise to drop this Spy Lady business, whatever it is, right now!"

This remark was not at all surprising, of course, as portraying just such a person was obviously part of the Spy Lady's operation and only went to prove how good she was at her profession. However, we promised at once as we did not want to upset Fthr. any further and because as it was so dark he would not be able to see that we kept our fingers crossed.

We were by now half across the bay, and it was at this point in time and sea that the aforementioned tragedy occurred which it is now my sad task to relate.

"My honey clam!" Rachel suddenly shrieked. "Oh, my poor honey clam's overboard!"

Thus the first we heard of the drama was also the last, the beginning of the calamity, its own end. The honey clam, resting at Rachel's side one moment as she sleepily reached to pull the blanket around them both more tightly, had the next moment by a sudden swerve of the boat been swept into the sea.

"My honey clam!" sobbed Rachel and, stricken, we all took up the cry. Father cut the motor and we searched the water back and forth, and Ham even dived down to look around with the underwater flashlight until Fthr. finally made him get back into the boat. It was hopeless, of course, and we sadly continued across the bay to Hamsterdam, looking perhaps like an ordinary Cape Cod skiff but feeling like a Venetian funeral gondola. Rachel wept inconsolably, and to tell the truth, the rest of our hearts were heavy and burned with the guilt of that very day's clam chowder.

As soon as we got home, we lowered the S.S.F.T.D.A.S.-O.C. flag to half-mast and solemnly pledged that every day at low tide, when all the mollusks come sucking up for air, we would give a moment's silent thought to the memory of the honey clam.

Before he went to sleep, Ham made up the following poem for Rachel, and I think it is the best tribute with which to end.

A Honey Clam from Hamsterdam
Went sailing out to sea
To try to get to Snailsport
In time for scones and tea.

She ran into an Octopus
Who tangled up her feet
And drugged her down to greeny graves
(She never got to eat).

The Arrival and
Untimely Departure of
Mad Sophie and Others

The plot thickens like a bowl of pudding. The true meaning of the Spy Lady's mysterious telegram is now known. A complete report of our new Intelligence, including its unofficial source (Oma) follows at once.

Time: Early this morning
Place: Breakfast

We four sat half asleep at the table until Oma spoke out from the kitchen, whereupon we sprang awake, for her words were as startling as a bugle call at dawn.

"You know our French lady next door?" she said. "Well, now there are two of them there."

We gaped, speechless, at one another as the awesome vision of the Spy Lady splitting amoeba-like at night and multiplying until she filled the harbor went through our heads.

"Two of them?" Squid repeated, choking on his toast.

"Are you sure?" said the Arab.

"How not?" replied Oma, shoving the bacon through the hatchway. "I was right there when the red-headed one came, wasn't I?"

"The red-headed one!" the Contessa and I echoed.

"You were there?!" said Squid.

Oma came round into the dining room and stood with her hands on her hips, giving us a keen looking-over.

"What are you, parrots, today? And what is so marvelous anyway that she gets company next door like everybody else? Except this one arrives with the Milk Man and so comes earlier than most."

"She came with the Milk Man?!" said the Contessa.

"Not in the same truck, no, but at the same time," Oma said, and clucking impatiently at the English language, she briskly enacted the scene, as she can move in quite a lively fashion for one so bulky.

"I am here, you see, standing by the milk wagon like this: should I, yes, get cream for whipping because this afternoon comes the Strawberry Man or no, when Squeak Slam up pulls a taxi who stops not two inches from my backside! I jump like so! and look, naturally, to see who is running me over so early in the morning. And there in the back seat sits The Company with gold hoop earrings so big they could have come rolling up the street by themselves instead of sitting in a taxi with her. Bit by bit she unravels herself from the taxi, and finally she is out bag and baggage. Now I see she has a mop of red hair and is wearing a linen coat the color of lemon ice. And so active she is, like a windmill. With one arm she waves away the taxi, and with the other she begins pounding at the house.

" 'Hallo, Good Morning, Where are you?' she calls through the door and up at the windows. *'Bonjour,* Wake up, *C'est moi,* I am here!' she shouts in a voice like the sun announcing herself. 'It is me, Madeleine Sophie!' "

"Madeleine Sophie!" we cried, looking at each other in astonishment.

"That's just what the other one said," Oma commented. "She opened the door a little way, still asleep in her long robe with her hair hanging down. 'Madeleine Sophie!' she says."

Squid waited, eyes narrowed thoughtfully, until Oma had gone back in the kitchen, and then he leaned across the table. "Meezleezleteezle azeczleteezle Peezleozeezleseezleteeze Threezleezle," he said in a low voice, although not low enough as Oma's head came poking through the hatchway.

"You call that good English?" she demanded. But nobody replied as by then we were already at Post Three, an odd hollow under the living room staircase, as that was the nearest secret meeting place.

Summary of Special Meeting at Post Three

This account is written from memory alone as the Secretary could take no notes due to the dark, crowded, and excited atmosphere under the stairs with everybody squealing out of turn like a run of pigs despite the President's shoves and kicks for Order.

The first thing we did was to get out the Spy Lady's telegram, and even by flashlight you could see that Madeleine Sophie clearly meant Madeleine Sophie.

"That still leaves us with Lehman Dash Chottley," the Arab pointed out, but it didn't really, for we quickly saw that if she used two names to start with, the others in the telegram must be hers as well. Including even the Dash or—.

"Madeleine Sophie Lehman-Chottley," Squid said, trying it out. "I guess it works all right."

"I won't say I told you so," said the Contessa, "but I did, didn't I?"

"If I had a name like that," the Arab reflected, "I certainly wouldn't go telegraphing it all over the country."

"Don't worry, you wouldn't have a name like that. No more'n would she. It's obviously a fake," said Squid.

"Then why does she want to waste good money telegraphing it?" the Contessa asked.

The answer to this, though sinister, was obvious. It must have been sent as a calling card, and although I suppose it could be said that one spy doesn't make a ring any more than one swallow a summer, there is still little doubt that Madeleine Sophie Lehman-Chottley can be anything else but. A spy, that is, not a swallow.

"But if she's only another agent," the Contessa said, "then why wasn't the Spy Lady more happy to see her?"

"Maybe she's a double agent," the Arab suggested.

Squid then said we had better not waste any more time talking but get to work, and he quickly planned the morning's Operation. It's true, even if he says so himself, that he did some pretty clever figuring. It is reproduced below by popular request (his).

"It is a fact that Spy Ladies are all natural-born actresses and, in order to give people the wrong idea, act the opposite of what you'd expect them to do since otherwise they'd give the whole thing away. It is also a fact that the tide is now all the way out. It therefore follows that the most (un)natural course of action the Spy Lady and Madeleine Sophie Lehman-Chottley would take would be to pretend that all they are is the same as everybody else in Scrimshaw: Hostess and Guest, and since when the tide is all the way gone all Hostesses take their Guests for walks out on the flats, this is the best place for our men, who will be Eustacia and the Arab because it's their turn, to lay in wait for them."

The meeting was then adjourned and just in time as this was Mrs. Cook's cleaning day and she had already started nosing around under the stairs with the vacuum cleaner.

The Arab and I hurried off to prepare for the assignment, and since we would have no cover or camouflage but our own, we took special care with the disguises. The final effect was I believe quite good. In fact, had we not been already related, I am not sure that even we would have known who we were. I borrowed Oma's navy blue bathing suit as it is a good quiet color, only then in order to fill out all the important places, I was obliged to filch the sofa cushions as well, which was not so easy. I also wore the Cleopatra wig with a false nose and mouth, plus a large pair of sunglasses to be extra safe. As for the Arab, he had on his neat black bowler, new eyebrows as big and furry as a pair of caterpillars, large glasses with eyes, and a fake cigar that you can blow smoke out of, although also fake.

We armed ourselves with Portuguese bread, as feeding

the sea gulls was to be our subterfuge while we waited for the Spy Lady and Co. to appear, and headed out to the sandbars. Icarus came hurrying after us, and although he wasn't in the original plan, we let him come along anyway since he hardly ever gets a chance to meet any of his own kind. Not, I might add, that it did any good, for despite the Arab's hope that Icarus would pick up a few pointers about taking off and landing, he paid no attention to the other sea gulls whatsoever but merely waited behind us, pacing impatiently like a stout little tourist anxious to get on with his walk. I suppose he must be the only one who has never heard that birds of a feather gather together, although I cannot pretend to be sorry as the sea gulls' loss has certainly been our gain.

We waited for quite a while and were just beginning to worry lest we should run out of bread when finally we espied the Spy Lady and Madeleine Sophie Lehman-Chottley (hereafter referred to in the records as Mad Sophie, which beside being more abbrev. happens to suit her v. well as will be seen) come promenading out on the flats just as Squid had calculated.

The Arab and I moved in on them. Not directly, of course, but like horseshoe crabs we pretended to look elsewhere, meanwhile advancing upon them in a steady sideways manner. This way we got our first good look at Mad Sophie who is the kind of person it is easy to see even from the corner of your eyes. Maybe even easier. She is tall, wide at the bottom and going narrower all the way up, which I think quite an odd shape unless you are a pyramid or something, but the Arab says it is a very practical design for a secret agent since for one thing it would make her almost impossible to knock over.

We sneaked up closer, pretending to hunt for objects like moon snails and sea worms except for Icarus, of course, who wasn't pretending. It was easy to see what Oma meant about Mad Sophie being a windmill. She was v. animated and kept flinging her arms all over the place, although I have to admit she was doing an excell. job of acting her role of Guest

"Oh, smell that sea air! Isn't it delicious?" she cried, whirling herself into a little tidal pool.

"Don't step on the minnows," the Spy Lady replied in a low voice.

"But what a marvelous place! Really, T., I should like to stay here forever," Mad Sophie gushed on, referring I guess to the whole of Scrimshaw and not just the pool, which was pretty slimy and full of Deadman's Fingers.

Now that we were closer, we noticed several odd things going on. One was Mad Sophie's voice. It, in fact, went on and on, a strange, fast nonstop voice with deep chortles in it, like a gunned-up motor. The Arab later said she sounded like she runs on more than earth oxygen, and went on to suggest that the S.S.F.T.D.A.S.O.C. might be dealing with a case of Interplanetary Espionage. I said I thought that was pretty farfetched (joke), but despite it is only a surmise and not anywhere near a fact, I am duly recording it because he insists.

Our other observation had to do with the Spy Lady who seemed to be oddly fidgety in Mad Sophie's company: e.g., digging around in the sand with her feet. Squid said maybe she was showing off and clamming with her toes, but that's ridiculous as she isn't that type at all, and it is my belief that Mad Sophie's arrival has definitely unnerved her.

I now come to the most important part of this Operation. For that matter of any of them so far as it is our first real proof of espionage, falling as it did from the Spy Lady's very own lips. In fact, we could hardly believe our ears and stayed riveted to the spot, which happened to be bent over face to face with a fat jellyfish, which is a lot closer than I usually like to stay.

94

Mad Sophie: Splendid, that lighthouse, and I suppose it comes in handy, doesn't it? Very clever of you, old girl, to have found a place like this. Yes, I would say Scrimshaw was the ideal spot and certainly worth the trouble one had tracking you down, my dear.

Spy Lady: (pause) It is very good here for my work.

Mad Sophie: Exactly. And I must say, T., I do think it's very sporting of you to be back on the job. I mean you did rather get slaughtered over your last piece of work, didn't you?

Spy Lady: Yes. (pause) But happily these scars do not show.

The Arab and I, still bent frozen over the jellyfish, waited with bated breath for more, but the next thing we heard was Good Morning and, looking through our legs, saw that despite we were more or less upside down, she was speaking to us! We were, naturally, too horror-stricken to reply and in any case could not without dropping our wax teeth all over the place, so I bobbed and the Arab tipped his bowler and we sidled away as fast as we could.

It is now late at night, just how late I think it better not to put down in actual figures. Squid, the Arab, the Contessa, and I have just come back from a late watch on the Spy Lady's house, and I am in bed where I must finish today's entry before it becomes tomorrow's.

We have been working steadily on the Case ever since the other day when the Arab and I heard the Spy Lady admit her own self that despite getting slaughtered once (?!), her work has now brought her to Scrimshaw. Squid said this is half the battle won already as it was practically a confession and all we have to do now is find out what of. But that is easier said than done, for although we seem to be on the right track, we still do not know where we are going. Or, more to the point, where the Spy Lady's going.

"Or even where she's been, like yesterday when she was gone nearly the whole morning," said the Contessa who is in bed with me and the Log Book. She ought of course to be in her own bed but is here due to being scared to death.

"I am not," said the Contessa.

Not that I blame her as late-night watches can be frightening at the best of times, which this cert. wasn't.

"You're writing it all back to front again," the Contessa observed. "Ham's going to get mad at you."

"Not half as mad as I'm going to get at you."

But she is right, and so I will begin near the Spy Lady's sun deck, under the old dinghy where we four crept after today's lunch. Luck was with us, for we had only just burrowed in and focused at the peepholes when the Spy Lady came tiptoeing out on the sun deck. She glanced back once or twice v. furtively and then sat down and quickly began writing in her notebook.

"What she want to go sneaking around in her own house for?" mused the Arab.

"It's good practice," Squid said.

But I myself wondered if it mightn't have something to do with Mad Sophie who, in fact, came outside soon after and stood by the Spy Lady's chair, so startling the latter whose head had been buried in her notebook that she gave quite a jump.

"You don't mind if I join you, do you, T.?" Mad Sophie asked, and started in pushing all the deck chairs around so that they faced the sun.

"Persis?" I felt the Contessa's cold feet interrupting me. "What do you really think the T. stands for?" she asked sleepily, nor for the first time either.

"Trouble," I replied.

"I bet it's a beautiful name, sort of darkish, you know,

like she is," the Contessa continued, ignoring me, and I shall now do the same lest I never finish this entry at all.

Mad Sophie then did a queer thing we had noticed her doing before. She went around testing out all the chairs until finally she settled down in the one closest to the sun and sat there with her head tilted back at about a 45° angle so that it could exactly meet the sun's rays. Most of us thought this was naturally to get it sunburned, but the Arab, following his hunch about inter-galactic espionage, pointed out that she went about it a whole lot more systematically than most people, and said he wouldn't be surprised if there was more going on between Mad Sophie and the Solar System than meets the naked eye.

As for the Spy Lady she just sat there looking none too happy as noted before in Mad Sophie's company. Her notebook remained open but she didn't get a chance to write anything more, for if Mad Sophie never stopped looking at the sun on the one hand, she also never stopped talking to the Spy Lady on the other. Yet strain as we might, we could hear nothing but a steady murmur as her chair faced windward.

"She must be mapping out their whole campaign," Squid said.

"Wouldn't you think she'd at least give the Spy Lady time to get it all written down?" I asked.

"Not unless she's as stupid as you," Squid replied. "It'd be much too risky."

We crept closer with the dinghy on our backs, looking no doubt like some kind of centipede crossing the sands, but still couldn't hear what Mad Sophie was saying.

"There's only one solution for breaking this sound barrier," Squid finally said. "We'll have to send a team over there."

We hurried back to Hamsterdam, where the Arab flipped his old Italian twenty-lire good-luck coin to see who would get the assignment. The Contessa and Parvis won, which as it turned out was about as far from lucky as you could get.

"I don't think that's a very nice thing to write down," the Contessa complained, flouncing around in bed beside me.

" 'Remember that the log-book is a legal document.' And that means the truth and nothing but the truth." Which I shall now continue with despite all obstacles, such as Rachel, lying in my way.

The Contessa quickly changed into her Gypsy rags and bangles disguise, but then we had to locate Parvis for the job, which was not so easy. We worried at first since it was Friday that he might already be up in the village drinking, but then the Arab heard him snoring and found him sprawled under the dining room table, fast asleep from all the broiled liver sneaked to him at lunch. Finding Parvis, however, turned out to be as nothing compared to waking him. We shook and pulled and Squid even blew his bos'n's whistle, but although Parvis finally opened his eyes and even rolled them around a little, we couldn't get him to stay up on his feet.

"Are you sure he's not drunk" Squid asked.

The Arab pulled Parvis's hair out of his face and sniffed at him.

"Only on liver and onions," he reported as Parvis gave another wheeze and sank back to the floor.

Squid tugged at him. "Just look at you, Parvis Samuel," he fumed. "You're no secret agent! You're not even a dog! You're nothing but a big fat fur rug!" Which I have to admit he did look like at the moment, except of course most rugs don't have such sensitive brown eyes.

"Oh, my poor darling, don't listen to him. It isn't true," the Contessa sobbed, flinging herself down on top of Parvis.

"Now look what you've done," the Arab told Squid. "Now we've got two rugs!"

But Parvis, jolted awake by the Contessa, tossed his hair back and sprang to his feet. In fact, by the time we had got him into his disguise, a large Russian bear's head (papier-mâché), he was looking as alert and keen as ever.

The plan for eavesdropping on Mad Sophie and the Spy Lady was that the Gypsy girl with Bear (the Contessa and Parvis, respectively) would wander over next door, loll around at the bottom of the sun deck gypsy-like, and maybe even beg a little if they got the chance, since the S.S.F.T.D.-A.S.O.C. could always use the money, even from its suspects, or as the Arab put it, especially from.

But nothing, alas, went according to plan. As soon as Squid, the Arab, and I had got up to the top deck to cover the Contessa and Parvis, we saw they were already too late. The Spy Lady had gone inside, and only Mad Sophie remained sitting in her deck chair although not, as it happened, for much longer. Hearing the Contessa's tambourine, she turned away from the sun, saw Parvis trotting along in his bear's head, and with a scream like the Scrimshaw fire siren, she leapt up on the rail of the sun deck.

"I guess she don't like Russian bears much," the Arab said. The feeling was, of course, mutual, and following his nose for villainy (and fire sirens, for that matter), Parvis gave a deep growl and went charging up the sun deck stairs.

"Parvis, you come back! Come here this very instant! Heel, you bad boy!" the Contessa screamed imperiously, but as she was using her Gypsy accent, nobody could understand her, least of all Parvis. Growling through his bear's head, he rushed at Mad Sophie who, still screaming, teetered on her rail and probably would have gone clear over bay-side if the Spy Lady had not just then come running out.

"It's all right, Madeleine Sophie," she called. "It's all right."

"Oh, no, not again!" cried Squid as the whole awful scene took place below us with words later supplied by the Contessa.

"I don't believe it. That stupid dog's done it again!"

For the moment Parvis heard the Spy Lady's voice, he screeched to a stop, turned around, and hurled himself into her arms, nuzzling her joyously with his great bear's head.

"But it is all right, really," the Spy Lady told Mad Sophie who still clung to the rail. "Don't worry. I know him and he is not really such a bear, this dog. In fact, do I remember correctly, the last time we met he was still only a rabbit."

"That does it, all right," Squid moaned when the Contessa and Parvis had finally got home, which took a while as the latter kept on prancing around the Spy Lady like a mad thing. "That certainly does it. What a fiasco. She's broken right through Parvis's cover."

"Well, at least it proves your theory about her supersonic perfume," I said.

"I've been thinking about that," said the Arab, who had in fact been quietly sitting there thinking. "The way she goes around like that, all prepared for disarming canines, she must always have police dogs on her track. I mean, it could signify she's a lot more dangerous a spy than we ever thought."

"True," said Squid, cheering up a little. Only then he took another look at Parvis, stretched out and still panting like a Russian bear who'd been up dancing all night, and got v. glum again. "He's going to have to come off the Case, that's all there is to it."

"Poor Parvis," said the Contessa. "It isn't his fault."

"I never said it was. I only said now the Spy Lady's recognized him, he's got to come off the Case."

"Poor boy," I told Parvis, who was already making the rounds of the room as the one thing he likes next to compliments is sympathy.

The S.S.F.T.D.A.S.O.C. then decided in favor of holding a special night watch on the Spy Lady's house in the hope of making up for this last failure.

"We'll have to borrow some coffee from below," Squid said, "so's to be able to stay awake late enough. In fact, the later we start the watch, the better."

"Why?" asked the Contessa uneasily.

"Elementary, my dear Contessa. Such as it's a well-known fact how most people change into their real true selves after dark."

"I can't think of anybody but Dracula and Dr. Jekyll and Mr. Hyde," said the Arab.

"Exactly," replied Squid with an enigmatic smile.

The room went strangely quiet, and the Contessa's rosy cheeks faded away.

"They're not facts, anyway," I pointed out. "They're fiction." But I do not think I convinced anybody, least of all myself.

As planned, it was about 2230 by the time we took up our position and much darker out than we had expected. It was also oddly still, as though everything were sneaking around on tiptoes including the night itself.

We stayed low behind the breakwater and watched the Spy Lady's living room window wherein she and Mad Sophie were framed. Only the latter, however, was clearly seen as she was facing out, but this gave us a good opportunity to study her face some more despite the fact it was again (still?) in motion.

"I don't think she looks much like a Spy Lady," the Contessa said.

"If she's working for another planet, she wouldn't necessarily," said the Arab. "Or maybe she's only assuming a human spy lady form and they botched the job up a little."

Somewhere over the bay a sea gull screamed.

"I think we ought to go home now," the Contessa whispered.

"Not yet," replied Squid, pulling her back down, and just in time, for at that moment the Spy Lady jumped up to answer her telephone.

"Quick, Eustacia, put down the hour," Squid said.

I did, 2245, although this fact is less a clue than another mystery, for who would be calling the Spy Lady at this time of night and why? When she got back to her chair, the scene continued as before, with Mad Sophie's lips moving a mile a minute and the Spy Lady sitting quietly listening. After a while, however, the latter began checking on her wristwatch every few minutes, first just glancing down at it, then shaking it a bit, and at last holding it up to her ear.

"I guess she is pretty tired and wants to go to bed," said the Contessa who was and did.

"Don't be silly," Squid replied. "She's no baby like some people. Anyway, I doubt it's even a watch. It's probably a short-wave radio receiver.

But we had no further time to study this detail, for just then a searing white light came flashing down from the sky. This was not so surprising, of course, as who has not seen an occasional comet falling past? I do not mind admitting, however, that we were pretty shaken when a second one came hurtling down even closer to us than the first.

"Shooting stars!" cried the Arab. "What've I been telling you?!"

The Contessa huddled under my windbreaker. "Are they aiming at us?"

"Maybe not," Squid said, "but I don't think we ought to wait around to find out!"

Nor did we, and that ends today's entry, which is a good thing as Rachel keeps on kicking me even in her sleep. I have just decided though that I will let her stay anyway as I believe it is true about safety in numbers even if one of them is only an 8.

INTERRUPTION

There has been, as shown above, a blow to the very heart and machinery of the Secret Society For The Detection And Solution Of Crime. Nor was it a brief and passing thing, but a terrible interruption lasting five entire days although, as will be seen, this was a light sentence compared to what it would have been if luckily the interruption had not itself got interrupted.

During this period our investigation of the Spy Lady & Co. was so badly hampered that we barely limped along, which was double bad luck as what intelligence we did manage to gather was v. suspicious and getting more so.

Mad Sophie is still here, and despite she is as busy as ever sitting or lying under the sun, she almost never lets the Spy Lady out of her sight, nor has stopped talking at her. The Arab says it's looked to him like counter-espionage all along, and Squid thinks Mad Sophie must be trying to brainwash the Spy Lady. It cert. seems that way as among other things she has even got her stopped working on her notebooks. In fact, all that the Spy Lady does is listen to Mad Sophie and/or pace the deck. Except for when she occas. sneaks off. Yesterday, for instance, she managed to slip away in her Bentley, which was curious as all the further she sneaked to was Oyster Lane, which is right around the corner from Fthr's studio and a mere two-minute walk from here! So was taking the car just up the street a ruse to throw Mad Sophie off the track? If so, where was the Spy Lady really as when the Arab spotted it, the car was just sitting there parked and empty. Had the Spy Lady gone to meet a *third* agent? We are beginning to suspect Yes as several more telephone calls were observed coming in and one going out. We know the latter wasn't just an order to Nickerson's Grocery either as she was whispering very low and old man Nickerson is already deaf enough to begin with. Can the spy ring be widening under our very noses?

Worst of all, the interruption was such that until now I could not even, for security reasons, risk putting these few observations and remarks into the Log Book. It would not have been safe. Nothing was.

I had not planned to do more than show where we got interrupted as why go through a bad experience twice? But Squid and the Arab who just went by got all excited because of the Log directions up front mentioning about records being accurate and complete and all that about steering a true course. I pointed out to them where it also says, "The effect of leeway is a variable quantity best determined by experience and the navigator's judgment." However, as they are too young or dumb, probably both, to understand, there now follows an Account of the Interruption, and I hope they are satisfied.

The first we heard the bad news was already too late to be a fair warning. We were all at dinner, even Fthr. who had got back from the studio early. He had scrubbed off his clay, etc., and was even shaved and smelling nicely of some kind of lime lotion I never even knew he had.

Everybody was in a v. good mood despite there were baby lima beans, which ever since she was little have upset Rachel as she always starts in worrying about what happened to the mother. This night, though, except for refusing to eat them as usual, she partook of the general merriment, as did Father. In fàct, Fthr. was in quite high spirits as he has been lately, which hardly ever happens when he is in the middle of work and must mean the new sculpture is going unusually well. Not that we will ever know until he's done as he is a very fussy and secret artist and will never let anybody look until the very end.

Now just as I was remarking all this to myself, Fthr. chose to shatter our peaceful scene by tossing the following bomb into Oma's noodle casserole.

"Well, I bet nobody can guess who called me at the studio to say they were driving down for a visit?"

The dinner table plunged into silence as we felt such a terrible foreboding due to Fthr's voice (hearty) that nobody even dared to guess.

"The Nevilles!" Fthr. announced, and was met with strangled cries of alarm, for this, of course, had been our greatest fear.

"Tchtch," Oma said, shaking her head in the hatchway, although I am surprised to say her disapproval seemed aimed at us and not the Nevilles.

Squid looked the most devastated, and I knew he was worrying about how was the S.S.F.T.D.A.S.O.C. going to get its work done with the horrible Nevilles snooping all around.

"How long are they coming for?" I asked weakly, figuring we might as well get the worst over with.

"Oh, a few weeks, I suppose." This was certainly the worst all right, and Squid gave a howl, joined in, I might as well confess, by the rest of us.

"Good Lord, I've sired a pack of hyenas," Father sighed, getting up from the table. Oma started in tching again, meaning that she thought we were driving him away, but this wasn't true as he has a stronger stomach than that, which he then went on to prove.

"Come, come, children, a few Nevilles, more or less, can't be as bad as all that. In fact, it might be a pleasant change for you, having some children to play with instead of other bloodhounds." He then kissed Parvis good-bye and patted Rachel on the head although I'm sure he meant it the other way around and must have been more preoccupied than we thought.

"I've got a late sitting at the studio," he said. "Good night, my dears."

"What's he mean, late sitting?" Rachel asked as the door shut after Fthr. "I didn't know anybody was even coming for early ones."

But we had more than that to think about now, namely, the Nevilles. There are three of them supposedly, but the way they are always sneaking around and getting us into trouble, there might as well be a dozen. The biggest one is Marylynne which is written together but then has to be said separately in this southern molasses way she has. She's the mother but no better than the others. In fact, maybe she is worse as, being older, she gets away with more things, such as always trying to organize and redo everything around the house, especially us and Father. After her come Nathaniel, aged 12, and Marcus, aged 10. I will not dwell on their other shortcomings as I don't have the room. I will only mention that they are exceptional sneaks and bullies. As for their physical characteristics: Nathaniel is thin and Marcus is fat, and they both have very long, thin clamlike smiles which are all right for clams but look terrible on people.

"OK," said Oma, coming to the table where we four still sat, stricken. "Now you are going to listen to me. This time when the Nevilles are here, you will behave yourselves. No more tricks like the last visit, you here me?"

"What do you mean tricks?" said Ham in an injured voice.

"And so what do you call it, putting that terrible big tuna head with a nightcap into Mrs. Neville's bed? Oh, how that poor lady screamed."

"Well, how were we supposed to know she doesn't like tuna fish?" Jared said.

106

"I am telling you for the last time you must not always be making trouble with your Father's guests."

"We don't always," said Rachel.

"No? Then what is it when that little Hungarian artist your Father meets at the University conference comes for the night and right away his briefcase falls mysteriously into the bay? Some mystery."

"Well, how were we supposed to know it was only his traveling clock ticking like that?" Squid muttered.

"Oh, zoh?" said Oma. "And what then last summer when you chased away that nice Miss Gregory from the art gallery in Boston?"

"That's different," the Arab said. "Anyway, we never meant to chase her away."

"You expected her to stay, poor lady, after she almost drowns in her bubble bath from such a shock, to suddenly see the four of you and also the dog spying down the skylight at her?"

"But we thought she was mixed up with the Smugglers," I explained.

Oma puffed up her red cheeks and slowly let out the air. "Ouf," she said, "such wonderful reasons you always have for everything. OK, I'm telling you again: No trouble this time." She paused thoughtfully, which is always a bad sign. "Your Father needs friends his own age like Mrs. Neville."

"Marylynne's no friend," the Contessa pointed out. "She's his cousin."

"Twice removed," said the Arab.

"That's not far enough," Squid grumbled.

And he was cert. right about that as the following notes from the field notebook all too easily go to show.

Friday: M.&N.&M. arrived this aft. We were below deck
           but not far enough as Nathaniel found us right away.
           He has to wear glasses now, and it is really terrible to

think of him sneaking around and being able to see better. The S.S.F.T.D.A.S.O.C. must cover all traces of work or the whole Spy Lady Case could blow up.

N's glasses have big tortoiseshell rims, and he keeps taking them off for spit and polish in order to make Rachel cry, which I'm happy to say she hasn't yet done, although I can tell by her expression (miserable) she is all the time thinking of that poor tortoise.

Eve: What a disgusting fat litt. pig Marcus is. He eats everything in sight and then some, such as beating poor Parvis to his handouts under the table.

After supper the Arab heard Nathaniel tell Marylynne that he was positive something mysterious was going on as we had such nonchalant airs.

Later: Oma gave us mugs of hot choc. with vanilla sticks to take upstairs. We had just got settled into our beds when the peaceful bay night was rent by the shrill cries of what we thought was a gull in distress but turned out to be only Nathaniel who had not discovered until too late that his bed was already occupied by the Arab's red ants.

Sat.: Marylynne got up early on purpose to catch Fthr. before he left for the studio. She not only ate up all his blueberry muffins before we could, but made a big complaint about the Arab and his red ants, which was v. unfair as he had nothing to do with it. It was Squid and me.

Sat. Aft.: The S.S.F.T.D.A.S.O.C. took Nevilles to fish off Wharf except for me who was thus freed for patrol duty. Spotted Mad Sophie and Spy Lady on beach, the former stretched out under sun as usual, only seemed to be asleep. Not surprising as she must be getting pretty tired of all the talking, esp. late at night. After a while the Spy Lady tiptoed away and up Bay Street. Tailed her to sidewalk shell stand and hid in bush while she stopped for purchase and long talk with stand owners about the value of the sand dollars although I doubt they were more than six years old apiece. The owners, I mean, not the sand dollars. This is something I have noted before about the Spy Lady and think it is one of the reasons she is a successful secret agent. I mean most grownups talking to children either like to pretend you're as old as they are, or they're as young as you are. But not the Spy Lady who talks to everybody the same way and doesn't seem to be pretending about anything except, of course, that she isn't a dangerous spy.

As she left stand, felt a sudden clammy hand on my shoulder and stayed rooted with fear where I was on all fours under the bushes.

"Hey, Persis, what're you doing under there?" came this whisper belonging of course to Nathaniel who had sneaked back home to spy on me as I might have guessed. "What were you doing, anyway?" he persisted, his eyes looming up extra large behind his new glasses. "Were you spying on her or something?"

"Who?" I asked, and had to go on to pretend it was only the sand dollars I was interested in, although he wouldn't believe me, the beast, until I had gone and bought one for fifteen cents like any sucker tourist, which made the aft. a total waste.

Sat. Night: It is very late, but we have been awake waiting for Parvis to get home. He finally staggered back from the village a few minutes ago but jumped up into Marylynne's bed by mistake, whereupon the calm night was shattered by her piercing screams as she does not even like dogs when they are sober.

Sun.: Marylynne got Fthr. all dressed up and took him to a luncheon party. We felt very sorry for him but could not help as we were only four against one.

Mon.:   The S.S.F.T.D.A.S.O.C. hardly dares make a
          move. We are surrounded by prying eyes. This morn-
          ing Nathaniel was found prowling dangerously close to
          where the Log Book is hidden. The Arab and Squid
          removed his glasses as a protective measure, and I
          don't know why everybody made such a fuss as we
          planned all along to give them back.
Later: This being Marylynne's birthday, Oma made a
          special dinner, and we had to help with chores. Rachel
          set the table, and it looked quite splendid as she had
          managed to dig up some napkin rings. Even Mary-
          lynne was impressed, until she took her napkin out of
          the ring and saw it was really a fishbone. The ring, I
          mean. This got her v. upset, but I don't know why as I
          think it was pretty clever of Rachel to have thought it
          up, although maybe she could have cleaned out the
          marrow a little better.
              Afterwards Squid heard Marylynne tell Fthr. that we
          were growing up like a bunch of barbarians. Which is
          v. unfair as most barbarians don't even use napkins, let
          alone napkin rings.
Tues.:   Early this morn. the Spy Lady tried working at her
          notebook again, but Mad Sophie soon followed her
          out. For the first time in ages, the Spy Lady then began
          playing her violin, only much louder than usual. The
          Arab said she must be trying to drown Mad Sophie's
          voice. Squid said he bet that is not all she'd like to
          drown, the way she looks at Mad Sophie. Something is
          definitely wrong over there, and getting worse, we are
          sure, only what? Squid says the S.S.F.T.D.A.S.O.C.
          must find a way to resume full operation before it's too
          late.
Later: Our messenger service is temporarily out of order,
          poor thing, as Marcus fed him a piece of peppered

bread to find out if hamsters sneeze. When we finally caught up with M., we gave him a v.g. ducking in the bay although it was not easy as he is such a fat, slippery eel. Marylynne got hysterical because Marcus's clothes and shoes were all wet although how she could expect them to stay dry in the bay I am sure I don't know. Now Marcus is in bed with chattering teeth and we are in disgrace, which is the first peace and quiet we've had since the Nevilles came.

Wed: Marcus doesn't feel well and is still in bed. First Marylynne thought it was because of his sinuses getting soaked yesterday, but now she thinks maybe he is coming down with something that isn't even our fault.

Later: The Nevilles are gone! Marcus refused to eat anything all day long. I admit it was a surprise, and I'd have thought a nice one, but Marylynne didn't. She said, if she knew Marcus, which nobody could deny, it was a bad sign, and if he was getting sick, he'd be better off doing it at home. Which as it made such good sense, nobody argued with, least of all us.

END OF INTERRUPTION

For the past several days we have been working overtime on the Spy Lady Case to make up for the Neville episode. In fact, the Contessa and I are on duty right now even though it is nearly suppertime and the sun is going down. I am hurriedly writing up the Log, which until today I've not had time to do, whilst from under the deck we keep our eyes on Mad Sophie who is still, in spite of the late hour, lying on the beach. Squid and the Arab are meanwhile out tailing the Spy Lady who was spotted creeping from the front of her house while Mad Sophie was out back. The situation grows more suspicious. Something is definitely going on, or worse,

111

as the Arab says, going off. I know what he means as the
feeling is like watching a little flame slowly sizzle up a long-
fused bomb.

The first good chance we had to observe the Spy Lady
and Mad Sophie after the Nevilles left was also a bad one.
Totally unexpected and full of danger, it was made even
more perilous, as will be seen, by the Arab's blunder. Still,
he couldn't really help it as the whole encounter took us by
surprise, the occasion being social and not business. At least
not our business although it was, in point of fact, Father's.

Once every summer Fthr. sighs and groans and tells Oma
it's time to make the punch. Then he hides all his work in
progress and displays for sale all sculpture that isn't, and
opens his Studio doors to the general public, including us.
He says he must as it is a question of survival, but it is an
event he hates as it means he has to wear real shoes and
introduce people to other people, which is v. hard for him as
he cannot ever remember names. Once he even forgot his
own, but it was only his middle one, and anyway is so terrible you can hardly blame him.

This then is where we were, helping Father to pass
around the punch and names, when to our surprise and horror in walked the Spy Lady. She was wearing a deep pink
silk flowing pantsuit and, it must be admitted, looked quite
beautiful in her exotic foreign-agent way.

"What's she doing here?!" Squid gasped, spilling some
punch down the front of a guest to whom he was only supposed to be passing it.

"Look, Mad Sophie's here too!" whispered the Contessa
from her lookout hole at the top of one of Fthr's more abstract marble pieces.

When we had calmed down a bit, we realized that their
appearance wasn't so surprising after all since it is the custom for everybody in the village to stop in, from friends and
customers to mere passers-by, although to my knowledge we

had never before passed out punch to any spies, which is, of course, what threw us so off guard.

From where I stood (on Fthr's workbench) I could plainly see the Spy Lady's anxious and oddly suffering look as Mad Sophie caught up with her and, taking her arm, propelled her around the studio. It was harder to read Mad Sophie's face, for as usual she acted out her part of friendly guest and chattered and smiled as though nothing were wrong, but you could see how she kept a firm hold on the Spy Lady while her eyes darted around taking everything and everybody in. I then had to go back to passing out the punch and so observed nothing more until after a while Father, looking more cheerful than usual, though just as blank, of course, beckoned Squid, the Arab, the Contessa, and me to him. We started across the room and to our horror were halfway there before we realized he was standing in a small group of people among whom strongly numbered the Spy Lady and Mad Sophie. It was one of the worst moments in the history of the S.S.F.T.D.A.S.O.C., but too late to do anything except pretend we were only Fthr's children and let him introduce us to our very own suspects! Which is just what happened. Father got through the Spy Lady's name all right and even all four of ours, but when he came to Mad Sophie, he said, "And may I introduce—" and then his face got that wide-eyed, blank look and he came to a dead stop. If before I have described any other moment as the worst, I was wrong because this was the true worst moment of them all. The Arab, used to helping out at such difficult moments, opened his mouth and without thinking automatically supplied Father with the name.

"Madeleine Sophie Lehman-Chottley," he rattled off. There was a horrified silence (ours), but thank heavens nobody thought to ask him how he knew, although for one terrible instant the Spy Lady's eyebrows lifted with surprise and even Fthr. looked startled. Then after a moment, people began drifting away, including Mad Sophie, although not, to our dismay, the Spy Lady, who lingered on to talk. We closed in on Fthr., Squid and the Contessa on one side and the Arab and me on the other, as he had no idea of what was going on. Nor could wild horses have dragged us off to leave him alone in the hands of the Spy Lady. He, of course, knowing her only as Madame Symond next door, did not seem to even sense he was in any danger.

As it turned out, however, we might as well have saved our worry for ourselves as the Spy Lady mainly addressed herself to Squid, the Arab, the Contessa, and me, which as can be imagined made us pretty nervous.

"Has it not been such a beautiful summer," she said, looking straight at us with her wide brown eyes. "I hope you are having an interesting time?"

"Oh, yes," sighed the Contessa.

The Spy Lady then asked us some innocent-sounding questions about the Cape, clamming, and school, most of which we neatly sidestepped although it wasn't easy, up close to her like that. You have really to keep yourself on guard lest you relax in front of her bright smile much as a weary traveler by what appears to be a warm hearth. Which, of course, the Contessa kept doing and would have done altogether, melting like a snowman, had we not been there to kick her. Luckily she was wearing a dress for a change, which made it a lot easier to get her right on the shins.

Mad Sophie soon reappeared and some other guests came up to speak with Father, and thus the awful moment passed on as did the Spy Lady herself.

"Now there, Jonathan," I overheard an artist friend of Fthr's say, nodding toward the Spy Lady as she and Mad Sophie left the studio, "there is a head that ought to be scalpt." I wondered, startled, how he knew until Fthr. replied, and then I realized he had not said scalpt but sculpt.

"It already is," Fthr. said, referring I suppose to how well chiselled are her features, and that I am happy to say was the end of the encounter. Which recital I see I have finished just in time as Squid and the Arab are coming in under the deck and I am bound to be interrupted.

"What's been happening?" Squid asked.

"Nothing," replied the Contessa.

"What do you mean nothing?" Squid said so disagreeably it can only mean he and the Arab must have lost the Spy Lady's trail.

"Right," admitted the Arab, reading over my shoulder.

"Mad Sophie's still just lying there?" Squid asked, taking away the Contessa's telescope to look for himself. "OK, I'll keep watch for a while."

The Contessa is now sitting down next to me and popping seaweed bulbs, which will no doubt make Squid crosser as he hates the noise.

"How come Mad Sophie's out there so late?" said the Arab, and it's true. I mean that it is so late, for I can just barely see to write and must hurry and finish this entry before the light is completely gone.

The last thing I have to record is this morning's work, which is a v.g. example of how slowly the investigation is going. At 1145 the Arab spotted the Spy Lady answering her telephone. It must have been another of those mysterious calls as in the very next minute she sneaked out of the house and into her Bentley. Fortunately the Contessa had our bicycles ready, and Squid, the Arab, and I took off in pursuit. All the way up Bay Street the Spy Lady kept poking out the window to adjust her rear-view mirror, and the Arab and I worried that she had spotted us, but Squid said she was probably just making sure that Mad Sophie wasn't following her. We tailed the Spy Lady to the town parking lot and left the bicycles behind Mary's Bar and Grill. It was pretty clear from the telephone call and the way she kept glancing at her watch that she was hurrying to some appointment. But, alas, where and with whom we never discovered because just as she passed Town Hall, we saw Father coming down the street from the opp. way and so had to give up the chase, even though being pretty well disguised we might have got by him unrecognized.

Thus the Spy Lady's web grows into a thicker tangle, but woven of more questions than answers, which is a little discouraging.

"Right," agreed the Arab, back at my shoulder.

"Ssshh!" said Squid, who was still studying Mad Sophie.

For instance, if Mad Sophie was sent here to brainwash and/or sabotage the Spy Lady, how much longer does she have to carry out the assignment? And who is the Spy Lady's outside connection? There can hardly be any doubt left that we are dealing with quite a complicated case of counter-espionage.

"I think you better put down interplanetary counter-espionage just to be safe," said the Arab.

"Quiet!" Squid ordered. The Arab stopped talking, but the Contessa went on popping the seaweed, which echoed loud and empty in the growing dark.

"Ssssh, will you," Squid said hoarsely. "I think she's dead."

The seaweed dropped from the Contessa's hand. "Who is, Ham?" she asked.

Squid turned around, his face strangely white in the dusk. "Mad Sophie," he replied.

The Spy Lady and
the Muffin Man

The mystery expands like Oma's bread dough left out on a hot day, rising up everywhere, huge and shapeless. There is now at least one other agent as well as a corpse loose in town. We think he may even be the Head of an international spy ring. One thing certain: it was he the Spy Lady contacted after doing away with Mad Sophie. But I had better back up to the latter's remains, for like the dough I am getting all ahead of myself.

The Arab, the Contessa, and I stood there, too stunned to move.

"She's dead," Squid slowly repeated. "Mad Sophie's dead."

The Contessa gave a long, quivering gasp.

"Come on, Ham," I said. "That's what you always say."

"But this time it's true."

The Arab tugged his moustache. "What makes you think she's not just still sunbathing?"

"Elementary, my dear Arab," replied Squid with a hollow laugh. "There is no longer any sun."

This was true. It must have been close to 1830 by now. Except for us four under the deck and Mad Sophie on the sand, the whole beachfront was deserted.

"Pretty dead, eh?" Squid asked the Arab who was silently studying Mad Sophie with his binoculars.

"She sure looks it all right."

"Can I see?" asked the Contessa.

Squid made room at the underpinnings, and the Contessa and I focused our telescopes on Mad Sophie's beach towel. Her long brown body lay absolutely still on its stomach, the head rolled over to one side, the arms carelessly flung out.

"She looks to me like she's only sleeping," the Contessa said.

"That's just exactly what she's supposed to look like, idiot," said Squid. "Anyway, all you have to do is ask yourself this: If she's only asleep, then how come she hasn't woke up?"

"True," murmured the Arab. "It is getting pretty late."

"Right," said Squid, "and that's not all. There's a small but very important piece of evidence you're overlooking: namely, that horsefly hanging around her feet."

We quickly drew our sights on the bottom of Mad Sophie, and sure enough there was this horsefly hopping from one foot to another (hers).

"See that?" said Squid. "And you know what? She's never even twitched one toe the whole time he's been buzzing at her feet." He gave us a grim look. "And the only kind of person who's got no toe reflex—"

"—is a dead one," finished the Arab.

"Exactly. Or in this case, a murdered one."

The Contessa gave an odd little whimper, and my skin went prickly cold as these whispered words hung in the dark.

The Arab cleared his throat. "The work of the Spy Lady, I presume?"

"Naturally."

"How do you think she did it?"

Squid considered for a moment. "Slow poison."

"Arsenic?" I suggested.

The Arab shook his head. "Too old-fashioned. Nobody uses arsenic anymore. Especially if it's a case of intergalactic counter-espionage."

"That's right," said Squid. "It could have been some kind of delayed-action ray-gun that most of us earthlings never even heard of."

"She wouldn't do a thing like that," the Contessa gasped out.

Squid shrugged toward Mad Sophie's body. "Proof's in the pudding."

"I don't care," the Contessa argued, though in a v. shaky

120

voice. "She may be a Spy Lady and all that, but she wouldn't hurt anybody."

"Oh, I doubt it hurted," said the Arab. "Especially if it was some kind of secret cosmic ray."

A loud blast suddenly went off, and we four nearly jumped out of our skins before we realized it was only Oma on the foghorn for supper.

"So all we got to do now," Squid went on, "is get the Spy Lady's fingerprints off of Mad Sophie and we'll have the whole case wrapped up."

The foghorn blasted again, and the Arab pointed out that if we wanted a free hand to finish up the case by ourselves, we'd better go in as otherwise Oma might come out. This led to a discussion of postponing the examination of the corpus delicti until after supper.

The Contessa trembled beside me. "You mean go over her for fingerprints in the dark?"

"Of course not," Squid said. "We'll bring some flashlights and candles."

The supper summons went off again, so loud and noisy it could have woke the dead, and we hurried into the house. This, as it turned out, was our biggest mistake, for whereas rushing in was easy enough, getting out again was not. Fthr. fortunately was working late at the studio, but still so as not to arouse undue suspicion from Oma we had to sit down at the table in a natural way, although of course it is impossible to eat supper with a corpse on your mind, especially when it is boiled haddock. Supper I mean, not the corpse.

"What are you waiting for, the Blessing of the Fleet?" demanded Oma, duenna of the haddock, as she stood, arms folded, by the table to make sure we did right by her ward. "Eat."

But not even Parvis was willing to follow this order and treacherously left us with our hands stuck under the table, full of fish.

All in all it took a lot of time and ingenuity to get our plates cleaned off enough to get out of the dining room. We then collected powder and Scotch tape as Squid said he didn't see why it wouldn't take fingerprints off the surface of Mad Sophie as well as anything else. For security measures we left the house by way of an upstairs window and across the roof, although this proved a slow and perilous journey as the Contessa forgot to change into sneakers and kept slipping off.

By the time we hit the beach again it was close to 2000; a dark night with the moon clouded over. We followed Squid across the sand, hardly daring to breathe as he led the way to Mad Sophie.

"Get your lights ready," he warned as we approached the scene of the crime. "Now!"

We aimed our flashlights, which I do not mind admitting shook with nervousness as who likes to look a corpse in the face even when it is business? Only to our horror what we saw was even worse than what we had expected: Mad Sophie's body was gone.

"But it was right here!" Squid whispered. "It's got to be here someplace. Spread out, everybody!"

We quickly divided up into points N.S.E.W. and began to search, but staying within easy call of each other, which was a good thing as the Contessa soon did, although actually it was more of a scream. I have noticed before how much more frightening screams sound in the night, and to tell the truth we others were near to screaming ourselves by the time we reached the poor Contessa where she lay fallen into the clutches of a terrible bony carcass, which despite it wasn't Mad Sophie's but only belonged to some huge fish that had washed up on shore, was nevertheless just as dead if not more so. Why the Contessa did not simply get up and leave such company instead of lying there screeching was that she had no choice as her hair had got so tangled up in the skeleton that I began to fear we would never be able to pick her clean from the bones.

This was not, of course, a v. auspicious beginning to our search. Nor did it improve any, for although we kept on circling all around where Mad Sophie's body had been and even further afield than that, our flashlight beams crisscrossing the whole bay front, we never found a trace of her.

"Damndamndamn!" cried one of us, which I will not say but am transcribing the curse as it appeared since I do not see how anybody could blame him when you consider what a terrible loss such a large and important piece of evidence as Mad Sophie's body was.

"What could've happened to her?" Squid groaned.

"Maybe she just woke up and went in the house while we were at supper," whispered the Contessa.

"That's how much you know about murder," Squid replied with a bitter laugh.

"Maybe her body went back up to its own planet, then," sugg. the Arab. "Like how the Little Prince got back to Asteroid B-612."

"Maybe," said Squid, "but he's only a story, don't forget." He paused a moment and then, lowering his voice, said what nobody up till then had even wanted to think. "If you ask me, all this lack of evidence can only point to one fact: the Spy Lady must have come out and dragged Mad Sophie off."

"Where to?" said the Arab.

"That's for her to know and us to find out," Squid declared, and squaring his shoulders, he resolutely started for the Spy Lady's house, the rest of us following single file behind him, although not nearly so squared-off in the shoulders.

When we got within sight of her living room window, we saw it was open due to the warm night and, throwing all caution to the wind, crept through the shadows until we got right up under it. It was well worth the risk, too, for Squid's hunch proved to be excell. and although it did not exactly lead us to Mad Sophie's body, we came away with something almost as good.

Telephone:　(ring)

Spy Lady:　*Allo?* Oh, it is you? *Ciao.* (pause) *Mais, non,* it is perfectly all right. Me, I am quite alone.

Ah, *oui,* she is gone, Madeleine Sophie. But not, unhappily, without first a little (throaty chuckle) assistance. *Comprenez-vous?*

Oui, it was quick. But, naturally, I had everything ready for her in advance.

Ah, *oui,* it was unavoidable. There was no other way. One had to protect oneself, one's work.

Oui, oui. Still, at such delicate times, one feels a little badly, *n'est-ce pas?* After all, we did once work together however long ago. I did not want, you know, to be unkind, to hurt her. (sigh) Yet it could not be helped. I had to get rid of her."

Her last words hit the air like shots in the night and so, to tell the truth, did we, although despite how fast we ran, our hearts like a bunch of scared rabbits were jumping ahead of us all the way home. In fact, if you don't count the Contessa's squeals, which get out by themselves like air from a bicycle tire, nobody even dared open their mouths until we were safely locked in my room.

"I can't get over it!" said Squid. "I mean you heard her—the Spy Lady even admits it out loud her own self!"

"It was as good as a confession," I said.

"Except for one thing," the Arab pointed out. "What's so great about a confession if you can't find the crime anymore?"

"Don't worry. Mad Sophie'll turn up," Squid said. "Like a bad penny. For one thing the Spy Lady didn't have enough time to hide the body that well. All we got to do is keep our eyes and ears open."

"And nose," added the Arab in his practical way.

"I wonder who was it on the other end of the telephone?" the Contessa said.

"Probably the same one as before," Squid said. "I mean the way she talked about getting rid of Mad Sophie, it's got to be somebody she really knows and trusts. He may have even helped her plan it."

"Also," the Arab said, "it was somebody who can understand French."

"Italian, too. Remember how she said *Ciao?*"

An awful silence settled on us while we considered what we had already begun to suspect even before Mad Sophie's murder.

"There's no doubt about it. There's another foreign agent somewhere out there," Squid whispered, nodding toward the window.

"If not more," added the Arab, and the meeting ended right there with the harrowing vision of ourselves ringed in by a nightful of spies.

Fortunately the next day dawned early. Despite the dark deeds of the night before, it was a warm bright blue morning, ripe with the smell of blueberries.

"Perfect hunting weather," Squid remarked as directly after breakfast we resumed the search for Mad Sophie's corpse, which as it turned out was far from perfect.

We picked up the trail where we had left off, at the Spy

Lady's house. This time we stationed ourselves behind the hedges near her kitchen door, and once again luck was with us, or so it seemed.

"There she is!" whispered the Contessa, and through the door we glimpsed the Spy Lady fully dressed and bustling about in spite of the early hour.

"She doesn't look very guilty or anything," I said as we watched her humming around with her coffeepot and all.

"That's probably the first thing she learned to hide," Squid said, "next to the evidence, of course."

"Sssh, look!" hissed the Arab, and as we watched, the Spy Lady put aside her coffee cup with a sort of sigh, wiped her hands with a paper towel, and came over to the closet near the kitchen door. A terrible premonition began to grow upon us as we watched her tug at the knob, so that when the door finally gave way and a large stuffed laundry bag fell out with an awful thud, I cannot say we were very surprised. And if we had any doubts as to the laundry sack's true identity, they were immediately removed by the Spy Lady herself.

"Oouf!" she gasped, trying to lift it from the floor. "She must weigh a ton, that bag."

"Mad Sophie!" Squid whispered triumphantly. "What did I tell you!" and as we watched, appalled, the Spy Lady dragged her terrible burden down the kitchen steps and over to the Bentley, where she heaved it into the trunk.

"*Voila!*" she said, slamming the lid down and in her haste catching a corner of the laundry bag. The Contessa flinched and, despite she knew Mad Sophie could feel no pain, would have doubtless cried out in sympathy had not the Arab quickly stuffed her mouth with his red bandanna.

"Quick, after her!" Squid ordered, and we dashed for our bicycles and set off in pursuit. Even the Contessa whose legs, the Arab warned, were too short, although what he actually meant, of course, was whose stomach is too weak as it gets churned up at the drop of a hat, let alone a head.

But the way it turned out, alas, the only thing that got churned up was the contents of the laundry bag itself. The Spy Lady, proving her great cunning once more, had led us on a wild goose chase that ended, of all places, at Seaman's Laundromat! where we pulled up just in time to see old Mrs. Seaman's daughter-in-law help the Spy Lady carry the laundry bag in from the car. Right away we began to suspect something had gone wrong.

"Oh, no!" groaned Squid as we peered into the window, for what the Spy Lady was dumping into the washing machine was a heap of dirty sheets and not Mad Sophie at all.

"We've been duped. Again," the Arab said as we sat behind the fence waiting for the Spy Lady to do her wash.

"I just don't know," admitted Squid, tugging at his beard. "Either she's a lot cleverer than I thought or we're a lot dumber." On closer examination neither of these possibilities proved v. reassuring. In fact, they were quite depressing as was the thought of once again having let the corpse slip through our fingers.

I am happy to relate, however, that perseverance, as Fthr. always says, does have its rewards, and so in the end the day was saved after all, for when the Spy Lady finished her laundry, we tailed her to the Town Hall and here at last espied the mysterious stranger who opened this section of the Log Book.

He was waiting behind a newspaper on the bench nearest the Portuguese Bakery, and when the Spy Lady approached, he jumped up.

"Eeeek!" cried the Contessa, so frightened her squeal got away before anybody could stop it.

"Imbecile!" Squid muttered, pushing her down behind the Art Cinema kiosk from where we watched. But I cannot

127

say I blamed her even if she had endangered our position, for the Spy Lady's contact (control?) was a truly sinister sight.

"He's the one on the telephone all right," said Squid, and of this there could be no doubt, for he looked even more like a foreign agent than the Spy Lady herself. He was tall and bulky and wrapped in a great trench coat out of whose pocket he now slyly withdrew a paper bag. This he proffered to the Spy Lady who peered inside and finally took out an object about the size of a small hand grenade, but as she then proceeded to take a bite out of it, we figured it must only have been some kind of pastry from the bakery.

As the Spy Lady and her control (contact?) were deep in conversation, we had good opportunity to study the latter. He is tall and has shoulders of such an unusual breadth Squid says they must have been esp. developed for tackling enemy agents. He had a brown cap pulled down low over dark glasses, and his only visible feature was a tremendous nose, hawklike in style. As for the rest of his face, it was covered up by big old-fashioned mutton-chop whiskers, handlebar moustaches, and a Dutchman's beard. He wore dark brown trousers, shiny black shoes, and a horrible pair of black gloves that he kept on all the time!?!

Special News Bulletin

Fthr. has just come rushing home from the studio, even as I penned the above paragraph. He hadn't even stopped to clean up and was all stuck together with bits of clay and v. upset because of a telephone call he had just received from Marylynne Neville. Squid says why bother with the Nevilles again since it's nothing to do with us, but that is not strictly true, and as it is so short I shall simply tack the message on to this entry, which is anyway finished.

What Marylynne said was, in a word, mumps. This is

what Marcus was coming down (up?) with and now Nathaniel as well.

Fthr. was very worried and called Oma to bring out some sour half-pickles and then lined us up with them under the light to test for any signs of said disease. This, of course, was pretty silly as we never get close enough to the Nevilles to catch a ten-foot pole, let alone mumps, and I am happy to report that we ate the whole jar of half-pickles v. comfortably except for Rachel who naturally got upset wondering what had happened to their other halves.

At 0730 this morning James hurried across my bed with the following memo from the S.S.F.T.D.A.S.O.C. Lost and Found Department.

FINAL NOTICE

MISSING OBJECT:	BODY
FORMER OWNER:	MADELEINE SOPHIE LEHMAN-CHOTTLEY
VALUE:	SEMI-PRECIOUS IF TERRESTRIAL
	PRECIOUS IF INTERSTELLAR

MUST BE BROUGHT IN TODAY

DEAD OR DEAD!!!

Thus with renewed vigor and determination we set forth once again to find the elusive corpse, for as the Arab said, it wasn't going to last much longer.

Squid still thought that the Spy Lady must have hidden Mad Sophie somewhere around the house, and suggested we search the yard for any signs of freshly dug-up earth. As the Contessa was the only one of us small enough to burrow under the bushes and shrubs, the job fell to her alone. The Arab gave her his new magnifying glass which is fog-proof and keeps a nice clean view even if you breathe on it by mistake, and while we others waited behind the Bentley, the Contessa crept off to work. She got through the flower beds all right and around the rock garden, but as she went under the lilac bush, the Spy Lady suddenly emerged from the house.

"Run for it!" Squid hissed, but it was too late, for the Spy Lady was already swiftly bearing down upon her.

"Ah, it is the Contessa! Good morning to you, Contessa!" she called out, sounding as though she was perfectly used to finding all kinds of nobility creeping around under her lilacs in the morning, which I guess considering her years of experience in espionage maybe she was. As for the Contessa, she was so startled she sat up on her knees, her wig slightly askew and her mouth open but fortunately speechless.

"I wondered as I saw you," said the Spy Lady, "are you fond of oranges?" Astonished, we saw she was holding one out to the Contessa. "It comes from Tunisia, this one," she said sweetly, "and is very red inside."

"I bet it is," grimly whispered Squid.

To our horror, a faint smile contorted the Contessa's fake mouth, and for an awful moment we feared that like Snow White she would take the fruit. The Arab gave a light warning whistle, and the Contessa, fortunately coming to her senses, jumped up and got away just in time.

After this incident we decided it was safer to stay teamed up. The Arab and the Contessa went to search along the beach; under sun decks and piers and behind the breakwaters. They took Icarus along with them to bring back any emergency messages, although he is so slow they might just as well have taken along one of the Arab's red ants. Squid and I stayed close to Hamsterdam and searched in the shallow parts of the bay and also kept an eye on the Spy Lady's house. She did not come out again but stayed working at her desk, although once or twice I saw her glancing furtively out the window in our direction. This worried me as I thought maybe she had spotted us, but Squid said it was normal behavior and to be expected as all guilty people imagine they are being watched.

130

By lunch time we still had made no breakthrough and so decided to hold a special meeting in regard to the mysterious disappearance of Mad Sophie's body and methods for its recovery.

But, "Zoh. This afternoon we go up to the village for shopping, the whole big bunch of us."

The above statement was issued by Oma through the hatchway at lunch, and thus we were forced to postpone our sorely needed meeting as we could not mutiny without arousing suspicion. At about 1420, then, we set out for the village, an account of which expedition now follows:

It was no exaggeration the way Oma referred to us as a whole big bunch. She is normally quite a bunch by herself, and when we all sail forth on narrow Bay Street whose tiny olden sidewalks I do not think were meant to hold more than one small pilgrim at a time, it is like the launching of an ocean liner with us a convoy of tugs.

When we are not in the middle of trying to solve a case such as the Spy Lady et al, we don't mind going with Oma at all as she is as fond of the Penny Candy Store as the next person. Nor was today any exception, and, in fact, it was here that Squid passed us a licorice stick with a hastily scribbled message inside.

"X is back," it said, and glancing out the store-front window, we saw yesterday's foreign agent come skulking out of the Portuguese Bakery and over to a bench.

"He must be waiting for the Spy Lady again," whispered the Contessa.

We watched as he cased the street, his head swiveling all around as easy as an owl's.

"You can tell he's a professional, all right," Squid said.

"What time is it?" asked the Arab.

"Almost 1525," said the Contessa.

"Put that down," Squid told me.

We then left the shop under cover of Oma, keeping a

sharp eye on the foreign agent. We figured he must be having a rendezvous with the Spy Lady soon as he kept glancing down the street and then up at the old tower clock as he dipped into his bakery bag.

"He's always hungry," the Contessa whispered as we crouched along behind Oma. "What's he eating now?"

"Looks like the same as yesterday," Squid said.

The Arab whipped out his pocket telescope. "Muffins," he reported. "Blueberry, I think."

We had by then reached Cook's Pharmacy, where Oma had to stop. After this we watched a sidewalk artist doing some tourist caricatures which actually were pretty flattering, and then went on up to the Crow's Nest Bookshop. It was now close to 1600, and as we started back, we saw a familiar figure in a black trench coat and hat go darting across the street.

"Look," whispered the Contessa. "There goes the Spy Lady to meet the Muffin Man." Which, of course, is just what we had expected, but more than that we did not see, for by then we were halfway into the Marine Surplus Store as Oma needed to get some ship candles and a knife sharpener, as, in fact, did we.

Below are the Secretary's notes from the S.S.F.T.D.A.S.-O.C.'s Special Meeting which finally convened after supper.

President: The meeting will now commence with a report on the state of the Mutual Fund.
Treasurer: Empty.
The Arab: This time last summer we practically had the Smuggler's Reward money in our hands.
President: The Weather Committee will kindly stick to remarks on the weather.
Weather Comm.:   Sunrise: 0508; High Tide: 0257; Low Tide: 0921; Temperature: 72 degrees; Barometer:

falling; Direction of Wind: East changing to Southeast. In other words, perfect conditions for whaling. That way we could at least get some money selling its teeth and things to all the tourists.

The Contessa: I just wish you'd leave those poor whales alone, Jared Samuel!

President: Order! for God's sake! This is an Emergency Meeting! And it's been called for one purpose only, which is to decide the best ways and means of handling the Spy Lady Case. The Secret Society For The Detection And Solution Of Crime is right now faced with a lot of sticky puzzle pieces involving a bunch of foreign agents, espionage of a still unknown nature, and, last but not least, murder. So what we got to do is fit them all together and see what the big picture actually is.

The Arab: Except one of the puzzle pieces is missing, don't forget.

Squid: Don't worry. That is the whole point of this meeting, to see does anybody have any further ideas on where the Spy Lady could have hid Mad Sophie's body.

Eustacia: We haven't tried the cemetery.

Squid: Too obvious.

The Arab: I have thought up a theory. Suppose you are stuck with a corpse on your hands in a little fishing village and it is summer and very hot. So where's the most logical place you'd hide it?

There was a few moments' silence while everybody turned sickly pale thinking where, especially the Contessa.

Squid: I think I've got it! On ice at the fish packing plant. Only it'd never work. Even the Spy Lady couldn't have ever sneaked her in past all those fish.

The Arab: Well, then, if you want to know what I think, I

133

still think the whole trouble is we're looking on the wrong planet.

Squid: That is as may be. But there are two people who know for sure what we are only guessing at.

The Contessa: The Spy Lady and the Muffin Man?

Squid: Exactly. And what I think we've got to do is concentrate on these two suspects from dawn to dusk because eventually they are bound to give themselves away. What I say is: Two spies in the hand are worth one corpse in the bush.

The meeting then concluded with the Arab making some identification sketches of the two principal suspects for our files. Once they were drawn out like that, side by side, it was easy to see what a perfect pair they make. These portraits also show what v.g. talent the Arab has for one his age as I think they are quite good enough to hang in any Post Office.

THE SPY LADY

THE MUFFIN MAN

The Unsolved Case
of Mumps

This log starts off two days back. Here's what happened. Woke up pretty d. sure there was somebody lying in wait for me. There was, too, but with luck it turned out to be only Parvis. Should have pretended not to recognize him, though, because he has this disgusting habit of kissing people good morning, and so naturally he came slobbering at me like some hairy old lady. The Arab says why complain, it's an easy way to get washed off for breakfast. Only what if that doesn't happen to be yr. native custom in the first place?

Checked out the morning: beach clear, sky empty, and bay calm. Could see all the way to Snailsport with one eye tied behind me. A typical *b.* day, which is the exact same type last summer's Smugglers were first spotted sneaking into the harbor. Sometimes wish they were back. Truth is, am beginning to suspect that smugglers are a lot easier to work on than spy ladies. For one thing they are more straightforward and dependable. Well, that's two things, so probably they're twice as easy. The Arab says this is no time to go and get discouraged, but I think it's the best one so far.

What I did next was usual morn. routine: assembled disguise, then polished all sizes spying lenses for the day's operation. Only it never took place because at breakfast Father grinned down mysteriously at his sausages and eggs and said, "How about all of us going fishing today?" It turned out he didn't mean them, though, but us, which was an even bigger surprise because he doesn't hardly ever like to be with people when in the middle of work. Conclusion? Obvious. Job must be going unusually well, probably nearing to finish. A good thing, too, because the way our business is going, I doubt we're going to be able to hand out anonymous financial aid to anybody, least of all broke sculptors with large families.

Returned from fishing trip approx. 1530. We got a good

catch, too, even though Fthr. let the Contessa come along, which was the usual mistake since all she ever wants to do is sabotage everything. You got to keep an eye on her every minute or she's tossing the catch back in the water or setting the worms free and lining the hooks with chewing gum so's none of the fish can hurt themselves. All the same I personally managed to get 5 mackerel and 7 flounder. But the best thing I caught was an invention called Back-Tracking Head-On. That's what I like about fishing: you just sit out there in the boat and pretty soon these ideas start darting into your head like a bunch of silverfish.

Here is a description of Back-Tracking Head-On. In the first place it is especially designed for tailing difficult suspects and is built around a disguise which is really an optical illusion. It works like this: the secret agent puts on all his clothes and hat completely backwards. He also wears a mask on the back of his head and covers his face with a long wig. This way he outwits the suspect by closely shadowing him yet always appearing to be going in the opposite direction.

By the time Oma had finished making me clean the fish for supper it was already 1640, but meanwhile the Contessa and the Arab had filed two reports in through the kitchen drainpipe. First the Contessa established that the Spy Lady definitely wasn't at home. Then the Arab reported as follows: "Left Tiddily's Grocery and spotted Muffin Man. Exact point was across from Father's studio in front of Pumper No. 5. He was sneaking up Bay Street and looked more mysterious than ever. In fact, you couldn't almost see him at all the way he had his cap pulled lower down and his collar higher up, etc. Lousy luck not to have any equipment on me. Thought about using Oma's new flour to get his footprints, only it wasn't the sifted kind."

I studied this new intelligence and made obvious deduction: the Spy Lady and the Muffin Man must be on their way to meet each other at Town Hall again.

This was correct except for one detail: where we finally tracked them down to was Greta's Coffee Shop. Got everybody stationed in front of the Fish Shack on opposite side of wharf with good view of the Spy Lady and Muffin Man's table through Greta's front windows. We kept watch, each of us using a large stick of cotton candy for cover, which I don't mind admitting was my idea. These worked pretty d. good since the telescopes went through nice and smooth and at the same time just by holding the pink globs in front of us we could hang around looking like we were nothing but ordinary tourists with cotton candy heads. Leastways that's what I figured until I saw that the Arab and the Contessa had been licking at theirs like a couple of idiots and didn't have enough cotton candy left to cover up even a shrunken head.

Lucky for them it proved not to matter too much since all this time the Spy Lady and the Muffin Man, being themselves no amateurs at the spy game, stayed behind Fat Greta's menus, which like herself are the biggest in town. Fact is the only two new clues we picked up from the whole bl. operation was that the Muffin Man took his coffee with sugar and the Spy Lady didn't, which we probably could have figured out for ourselves.

At approx. 1745 our watch was ended by a weird and mysterious incident. This incident was, in point of fact, Eustacia, whose face began smouldering like a hot coal behind the cotton candy.

"I'm sleepy, Ham. I want to go home," she whimpered. I was so surprised I nearly dropped my cover. I mean I couldn't hardly believe what I was hearing. But when I saw how she kept on sort of slipping down into her cotton candy, I began to think that something foul was afoot. The truth of the matter is I was getting d. worried because Eustacia is not that kind of agent at all. She isn't even that kind of girl. I mean for a female she can be as tough as the best of us, and so naturally fearing the worst, such as she had been secretly poisoned (cosmic ray or dart gun) when none of us were looking, I suspended the Operation and we quickly dragged her off home. It was a pretty grim scene, with the Arab looking like a piece of chalk and the Contessa dripping tears like the backyard faucet.

Oma and then Fthr. said she had probably got too much sun from the fishing trip, and we others would have liked to have believed it but hadn't much hope. By 1830 Eustacia had gone right off to bed and likewise to sleep without wanting any supper, not even the dessert.

Assigned everybody, including Parvis, to night watches over Eustacia so's we could keep a check for signs of life or anything elsc. Went on duty myself at approx. 2330. Didn't detect anything unusual except that she kept on tossing around and throwing off her blankets, which seemed to be a good sign. At least it looked like she wasn't going to give up without a pretty d. good fight. Left Parvis in charge at 0245. All in all it was a long night, but after a while it got over with and so did the suspense about what and/or who had struck down Eustacia.

Here is what happened. At about 0600 woke up and sent James over to Eustacia's room with a health chart, but then heard nothing from either of them. Next tried to contact Eustacia over the intercom, but the can-phones might as well have still been full of chicken soup and noodles for all the help they were. Swiftly went to investigate matters myself and encountered a most peculiar sight. There was Eustacia still flopped back on her pillow, not moving a bit, while James jumped up and down beside her, having a hysterical fit. I never saw him so mad. He kept getting up on his hind legs and screeching at Eustacia, and once I got a little closer

I saw what he meant. Her face was bulging like she had got up in the night and swiped his whole supply of food to store away in her cheeks for the winter. I mean I almost had to laugh because except that Eustacia wasn't little and furry, she looked enough like James to be his twin.

The Arab wandered in about then with the Contessa trailing behind him, and taking in the situation at a glance, he whipped the magnifying glass from his pajama pocket and went once lightly over Eustacia.

"A case of mumps, I'll wager," he declared, arriving at my very own conclusion.

Before calling in the house authorities, the S.S.F.T.D.A.-S.O.C. held a short meeting since I figured (correct) that there wouldn't be another chance for a while, and passed the following resolutions: (A) Not to ever leave our fellow agent and sister alone and unattended on her sickbed of pain, also in case she should get delirious and start blabbing and wreck the whole Spy Lady Case. (B) Seeing how we were now one agent short, Parvis would have to go back on regular duty case work. (C) The President would not mind taking over the duties of the Secretary, especially in the Log Book. The said Secretary offered no objection as it hurt too much, and so the meeting was concluded.

Quickly dispatched the Contessa to get Father and Oma, and they came running in and were pretty surprised to see Eustacia looking like a red balloon about to take off any minute from the pillow. The Arab who was getting hungry for breakfast offered to get out the pickle jar. But Fthr. sighed and said you didn't need any sour pickles now to see that poor Persis had caught the Nevilles' mumps all right. Then Oma tested her on the forehead and pulled her hand back like from off the stove.

"Ach, she is burning up with the fever, poor child," she said. This statement naturally set off the Contessa. I couldn't hardly blame her, though, because the way Oma

143

said it, it sounded like there maybe wasn't going to be much left of Persis except a few old ashes or something. Even Jared started in sniveling, only not as loud at Rachel. Or for that matter James who was still raising h. even though I had put him away in my pocket.

By now Fthr. had called up Dr. Adams, and he hurried right over and came puffing up the stairs with his old black bag, followed by Parvis and also Icarus, who was flapping all around the room so excited that for a while I thought he was going to forget himself and fly. It took old Dr. Adams a while to figure out which of us was the patient since nobody had got dressed yet and anyway he is so nearsighted. Finally he spotted Persis, and when he gave her his usual friendly chuck under the chin and saw she didn't have one anymore, he said the same thing as us others. Mumps.

It was very quiet at breakfast without Persis. We could hear her groaning some, but that wasn't the same. Nothing was the same if you get right down to it. We didn't lay eyes not once on the Spy Lady nor the Muffin Man and least of all Mad Sophie's body since there wasn't even enough time to dig up a new clue, never mind an old corpse. I mean between sick bay duty and running errands all over the place for Oma and also Father who stayed home most of the day, the S.S.F.T.D.A.S.O.C. was beginning to suffer nearly as much as Eustacia, and in actual fact took a def. turn for the worse that night.

It was about 2000 and everybody was upstairs except for Oma, who was still in the kitchen, and me, who'd come down to the living room to get Fthr. *Stories from Shakespeare,* which he always reads out loud whenever we're sick. So there I was, hunting through the bookcase next to the fireplace when suddenly I heard this sinister rapping at the window. I froze to the spot, positive if I turned around I would find a bullet (glass-proof) aimed to get me right between the eyes. The rapping stopped. Then it started up again, this time on the door, which was a little better, but I still wasn't taking any chances and stayed right where I was until Oma came in.

"What is wrong with you? You are suddenly such a big scholar with your head stuck in a book you can't even hear somebody at the door? Go and answer."

Having no choice, I did so, but slow and careful on the balls of my feet like me and the Arab trained to do in case we should suddenly need to spring. And did I ever need to, for when I eased open the door a tiny crack, who should be filling it up but the Spy Lady herself. And before I had recovered from this shock, she threw me into a worse one.

"I bring you this for your sister in case she should be feeling any better," she murmured in her strange deep voice as she pushed a jar into my hands.

"It is some fresh-made poisonberry jam," and with a sinister little laugh she vanished into the night. I could feel the blood draining from my head in a big rush, and I didn't blame it. I'd have run, too, if I could have, but as it was, I just stood there holding the poisonberry jam out in front of me as far away as I could get it.

"How sweet of her to do," said Oma, reaching from behind me and grabbing the jar as it was about to drop. "And you, what kind of big oaf are you? Your mouth stays open, everything goes in, and nothing comes out. You couldn't even thank Madame Symond for the boysenberry jam?"

"*Boysen*berry!?!" I gasped. "Did she say *boysenberry* jam?"

"Of course," Oma said, pointing to the label on the jar. "What were you expecting, more sour pickles?"

Well, that was a relief, all right, and once I thought it over, I realized that a cool and professional Spy Lady like her would be the last person to go around announcing her intentions in advance like that anyway. But then just as I began to relax, halfway up the stairs, a new and ominous thought struck me down: *How did the Spy Lady know about Eustacia's mumps?*

This finishes up what's been happening around here these past two days except for one final thing. That is an Amendment to Resolution (C) of the last S.S.F.T.D.A.S.O.C. meeting in which it says that the President wouldn't object to taking over the duties of the Secretary, esp. in the Log Book. Well, he's changed his mind. So the new Amendment reads that until such a time as the Secretary has regained her health and other writing facilities, all secret agents will from now on enter their own daily reports in the Log Book.

Squid

0900 Father let me carry up the yellow roses he got Persis. They are beautiful. I wish I had mumps.

  When I went in Persis's room, she was laid out very peaceful and natural if you don't count how funny she looked. I was pretty sure she was only sleeping, but I put a mirror at her mouth to make sure like Squid told us about and it worked.

Love,
Contessa

Love?! Are you out of yr. mind? What do you think this is, a pen-pal club?

1030 This aft. when I'm off duty, I'm going to try to invent a damp-proof hair. If whales had whiskers like walruses, that might be a good thing to use. This salted sea air is really bad for hair and can make it look like brillo in no time, even when it is human and expensive. In fact, after breakfast, found Oma trying to clean the frying pan with my good sou'easter's beard. Brushed and waxed it, also all other beards and moustaches, with Eustacia's toothbrush. Don't think she'll complain as she can't open her mouth wide enough. Put out all hairpieces to dry on roof, and that's how come I spotted the Spy Lady. She was going out on her sun deck and pulling this thing behind her. From the way she was tugging at it you could tell it was something pretty big. She finally got it through the doorway and out onto the deck, and all I have to say is it's a good thing none of our female agents were here or I'll wager they'd have fainted right off the roof. Because remember that big green empty trunk of hers? Well, that's what it was, except now you could tell it wasn't empty anymore but stuffed full with Mad Sophie. Or so I thought. True, I didn't know why she'd want to lug Mad Sophie out and open her up like Oma doing the spring cleaning, but I figured since it was such a nice morning, maybe she was going to air and mothproof her, which to tell the truth I never heard of, but it seemed like a pretty practical idea. Only then when she finally got the lid up, you wouldn't believe the mess in there—nothing but this big heap of shells and stones and sea urchins and sand dollars and starfish and all these old pieces of driftwood. I wonder is she trying to sneak off with the whole Cape Cod shore, or what?!

Arab

From now on all entries better be a lot shorter and more to the point if you know what I mean. For one thing the Log Book's running out of pages, and I think we ought to leave some for Eustacia since she is the official scribe after all.

Squid

1450   Rec'd. alert down drainpipe from the Contessa up on widow's walk: Spy Lady was heading for village on foot. Set out after her with Parvis. Tried out my Back-Tracking Head-On method for first time. Am not too proud to admit it was a big success. Spy Lady kept looking over her shoulder. Was getting more and more nervous to see no matter how fast she went, this other person (me) was still right behind her even though he was always headed in the opposite direction. Only slight hitch that developed was poor Parvis who also got confused by the disguise and kept trying to walk backwards to keep up with me. Finally he got so dizzy I had to take him back home.

Squid

1630   Father said Persis's fever is gone. We were glad about that and went up town to get her a present. We bought her ½ pound of saltwater taffy, mixed flavors, because that's all the money we had. She couldn't eat any, though, so we divided her share up, but she didn't mind.

Contessa

1045   If you want to know what I think, I think the S.S.F.T.D.A.S.O.C. might get a whole lot more work done if our patrol duty got better organized, say like the Coast Guard's.

For instance, me and Parvis shadowed the Spy Lady up Bay Street into village. Had to really move fast to keep her in sight. As she was hurrying past Town Hall, the Muffin Man came rushing out of Bakery. He was waiting for her with a note held out in his hand like a relay runner, and was planning to pass it to the Spy Lady and keep going. At least, that's my surmise. Will never know for sure because all Parvis needed was one look at the Muffin Man to sniff trouble, and with a wild yelp he went lunging across the street at him. Only here's the terrible part: once he got there, all he did was dance around him like a crazy nut and try to shake his hand!?!

The Muffin Man made a quick getaway, you can imagine, and disappeared into the crowd. So did the Spy Lady. The worst of it was when I got to Parvis, he was sitting there grinning and wagging his tail like he'd just met James Bond or somebody.

So how am I supposed to get any serious work done with Parvis along for a partner? I mean the way the stupid idiot was acting, I wouldn't have been surprised if he'd asked the Muffin Man for his autograph while he was at it!

Arab

Calm down and keep cool, will you? There's a simple explanation if you use your head: some of the Spy Lady's supersonic perfume must have rubbed off on the Muffin Man, that's all.

Squid

1130   Persis is better, only she still can't eat much be-
        sides soup. Oma said would I go up to Tiddily's
        to get some more, so I did. On the way back
        home, you know that little dead-end street up past
        Father's studio that has the good blueberry patch
        in it? Well, the Spy Lady was backing her car out
        of there. I thought Squid said the blueberry sea-
        son was finished.

                                                    Contessa

1520   Tailed Spy Lady to Bonsoir Cafe. She didn't ac-
        tually stop, only slowed down, looking all around
        for I guess the Muffin Man. Don't think she
        spotted me as I ducked behind the Moby Dick
        statue, and she quickly went on. She has been
        getting more and more jittery lately. You can tell
        by the way she keeps looking more behind her
        than in front of. Log records also show how she
        and the Muffin Man are rushing around a lot
        faster these past days, which could mean bad
        news, such as their plot's coming to an ugly head.
            Shadowed Spy Lady on to Crow's Nest Book-
        shop. She went browsing in far right-hand corner.
        This was no surprise since I knew before I even
        got out my telescope what's kept on those shelves:
        detective stories and spy books. What I didn't
        know was what was she after, pleasure reading or
        some helpful pointers? Naturally suspected the
        last. Waited approx. 45 minutes but she didn't
        come out, and so folded up my telescope and
        went in after her. Well, she wasn't in there any-
        more, and since she never came back out, at least

not the front entrance, it must've been helpful pointers she was after, all right.

Squid

2030   I guess Persis is really feeling better. Jared drew her portrait. It is called Girl with Mumps, and she tried to tear it up because she said you couldn't tell which was which.

Rachel

1045   Followed hunch and headed up on beach to scavenge since last night was pretty d. stormy and you can never tell. I mean there was at least a chance Mad Sophie's body might have washed up or something. No such luck, but then halfway up to the village sudden. spotted the Muffin Man scrambling down the old sea wall between the fish warehouse and Fthr's studio. Not the first time either that he or the Spy Lady has been observed sneaking around there. Advise all S.S.F.T.D.A.S.O.C. members to remain on extra alert for any signs of newly planted mines or explosives in this vicinity.

Shadowed Muffin Man all the way up to main wharf. He looked weirder than ever. He was barefoot and his pant legs were rolled up under his trench coat and his shoulders looked even bigger and his moustaches flapped away as he went rushing into the wind and through the low tide as fast as some kind of spread-winged sea bird.

The fact that he could go so fast barefooted and wasn't tripping and hobbling over the sea stones and bay glass like the usual inlander could

151

be an important clue as to his own native habitat, which I figured out must be some coastal region like maybe along the Iberian Sea.

Squid

1530   I wish Eustacia would hurry up and get all better. It is a very gray and rough type of afternoon. You can see the wind blowing the sea gulls all over the harbor. They are crying. I have been on the top deck watching the Spy Lady write in her notebook at the desk. She only got up once and came outside to gaze upward. Squid said she was probably expecting a signal. But I think she was worrying about the poor gulls.

Contessa

0900   This morning one side of Eustacia was gone, and when Father came in she had already finished off her breakfast and some of the Contessa's too since she had brought along a bunch of cereal to keep her company. Oma clapped her hands and said our troubles were over, but Fthr. said he thought it was more probably the other way around.

Arab

1630   I have just got home from tailing the Muffin Man and the Spy Lady to a bench in the village square. I don't feel so good either. I can't hardly even swallow. I guess that candy I ate was poisoned after all. Only I still think it's pretty silly of the Muffin Man to want to give poison chocolates to the Spy Lady when they are such good friends.

Squid thinks he must have meant it for one of us all along, but I don't see how because I saw him give it to her all wrapped up with a red ribbon. Squid said, "What did I expect, black?" But that's not what I meant.

Anyway then the Spy Lady and the Muffin Man must have heard something strange move in the bush (me), and they flew away and left the candy. I wish I had, too.

Rachel

2030   4 albatross egg whites
3 tbl. sea salt
½ pt. oyster juice
1 cup jelly of jellyfish
1 red-backed salamander tail
1 pair of fish eyes (boiled)
Stir briskly and sprinkle in some chopped-up kelp.

Arab

2100   What the h. do you call that?!?

Squid

It's an old whaling Captain's recipe for how to make an antidote to take after being poisoned. The Contessa wouldn't, but I figured it was a handy thing to have in the records anyway.

Arab

Hiatus

There has been a Hiatus although I am not sure that can be the right word since it sounds to me like an oasis of time in lovely bloom, which this certainly wasn't. Unless I am thinking of hibiscus, but of course it wasn't that either as the only thing in bloom during this interlude has been mumps.

Here is the latest Sick Call in order of those stricken after me: Rachel, Jared, Father, and Hamilton.

This is the first time I have been allowed to stay downstairs since the beginning of the Plague as Oma is v. strict and if you don't lie in bed by yourself, she will help you. She says she does not mind all the work as once when she was younger she was in charge of a Rest Room high up in the Tyrolean Alps that all the crowned heads of Europe came flocking to, which really impressed us until the Arab figured out she must mean Rest Home.

Parvis is the Night Nurse but naturally is not nearly so strict. In fact, he is very solicitous and worried as he doesn't know that mumps isn't a mortal illness and keeps on kissing the patients until he hears Oma come stomping up the stairs, and then he jumps down and sits there guarding the bed like a three-headed Cerberus.

Dr. Adams has been stopping by almost every day, but that is all right as it seems to be more to take coffee with Oma than our temperatures. Mrs. Cook the cleaning lady has been in and out a lot, too, although, unfort. I think more in than out.

Father's mumps came as quite a surprise, esp. to him. He has been pretty upset by the whole thing. I suspect it is his pride that hurts as much as his mumps. He keeps demanding to be let up and says it is damn stupid foolishness for a grown man like him to be stuck in bed with a ridiculous children's disease when he is so close to finishing up his summer's work.

Squid says exactly the same thing although he is even worse-tempered and keeps on swearing like an old sea dog but mostly under his breath as I guess it hurts too much to do it properly.

Oma has just come in to light the fire. It is quite a blustery night out, and I am curled up on the sofa in front of the fireplace with the Log Book whose last section of pages I am beginning to fill in. There aren't so very many left either, and, in fact, I am beginning to worry lest the Log Book gets finished before the Spy Lady Case. Which brings me to a new development in the investigation. I believe I have come upon a v.g. idea for cracking the case; at least the Mad Sophie part of it. I thought it all out while I was sick. It is quite a different ploy than any used hithertofore by the S.S.F.T.D.A.S.O.C., being perhaps more artistic and literary. But what it lacks in brawn I believe it makes up in brain, and so will work. I cannot write anything more about it now, however, as first I must tidy the Log and bring it up to date by copying in all the last reports that poor Squid and the Arab left scribbled on little odds and ends of paper.

Well, I guess the Capt's potion wouldn't have helped Rachel anyway since it turns out it was mumps and not poisoned chocolates that did her in. The way we found out was this morning when we heard Oma give a little scream and we went rushing into Rachel's room, and there she was lying in bed looking like somebody who'd swallowed a boa constrictor instead of the other way around.

Arab

Sighted the Muffin Man and the Spy Lady having coffee at Fat Greta's. They didn't stay long, but all the time they were there the Muffin Man kept scribbling over this paper map of Scrimshaw that Greta puts on all the tables to serve on top of. Waited till they left and ran in and snatched it up before the waitress got to it. Saw these zigzag lines along the border and got very excited, thinking, naturally, it might lead to where Mad Sophie's body was hidden. But then when I got a better look, I saw it was nothing but a sketch of the Spy Lady's profile!?! What a gyp, though I got to admit once you figured out what it was, it wasn't such bad work for a foreign agent.

Arab

Spied Muffin Man and Spy Lady walking briskly out on Wharf. Despite hot sunshine Muffin Man was wrapped up in this big brown muffler like an old Eskimo grandmother. Either he's trying to disguise himself even more, or he's got a stiff neck or something. Tailed them out to end of Wharf, and then the bl. Boston steamer unloaded all its tourists and they got swallowed up in the crowd. Looked everywhere, even down on the beach, but couldn't spot them again.

Went back by beach. No other news except found a big moon snail and took it home to cheer up the Contessa.

Squid

Nuts. Every time sleuthing takes me out, Oma has to think up more errands. Hate mixing business with work. She says it can't be helped since now that Father has the mumps, I'm the oldest man of the house. Worse luck. All the same managed to pick up Spy Lady's trail. Followed her to fish market on Wharf. Turned out to be a red herring, naturally. Must have thought she had given me the slip since she then hurried first to Stationery Store, where she bought 3 yellow pads, 2 erasers, and a notebook (so the paper work isn't finished yet!?), and then Post Office for 2 stamps (air mail international!?!). After this, turned around and went home. Didn't meet up with the Muffin Man anywheres today.

Squid

Well, now the Arab is down with the mump. The reason there is no *s* on that word is because he has only got this one big mump on his left side, which gives him a d. queer lopsided look like he is listing pretty bad and about to keel over. Which come to think of it is just what he did. Icarus has been perched on the Arab's bedpost ever since yester. He keeps up this awful worried mewing and once went out and brought back a little sand eel which he was trying to feed to the Arab, except Fthr. got there just in time. On second thought it wasn't such a bad idea since it's probably the only thing could have slid down past the mump.

I am getting pretty worried since this now means out of the whole S.S.F.T.D.A.S.O.C. I am the only one left standing on his feet. Unless you count Parvis and James and Icarus. Though now I think about it, I guess that's at least pretty many feet.

Spy Lady spent most of day working with yesterday's supplies. She didn't go up to the village at all to meet the Muffin Man. I did though, but didn't see him anywhere around.

Squid

Still no trace of the Muffin Man. This aft. tailed Spy Lady out to Wharf, where he was last seen in her company. She just stood there, searching out to sea. Beginning to suspect the Muffin Man might have made his getaway in a submarine or space ship. Something d. peculiar going on, that's for sure.

Squid

Shadowed Spy Lady up to village in rain this morning. Harder all the time since she's getting so slippery and is always checking around over her shoulder. Today took Oma's big black umbrella for extra cover.

Tailed her to Cook's Pharmacy and watched from behind the hair lotions. Couldn't believe what happened next. She leaned up close over the counter and said very low to the druggist: "Will you help me, please. I need something very strong—a spray perhaps —to get rid of some terrible little beasts." Got out of there as fast as I could. So for all our caution she has got on to us! That is not all this incident signifies either. It could explain the mysterious disappearance of the Muffin Man! Maybe Mad Sophie's body is not the only one missing! The S.S.F.T.D.A.S.O.C. must proceed on Red Alert, but won't tell the others that their very lives are in danger until they are better.

In fact, I feel terrible already.

I wonder can you get poisoned by osmosis?

Squid

That finishes the Arab's and Squid's notes.

I just went to look up what osmosis means, and of course you can't get poisoned by it, nor did he as naturally it was only the mumps.

Oma came in and caught me at the dictionary stand and started complaining how it was past time for me to get back into bed, especially if I was going to go standing around in

161

drafts, which I'm sure I wasn't unless she's counting the flutter of the dictionary pages. So now I will have to wait until tomorrow to present my aforementioned plan. But before I close up the Log Book for the night, I want to add on to the end of Squid's notes that his first theory about the Muffin Man going off by submarine or space ship makes the most sense as frankly I think she must have been referring to some kind of bugs as I don't see how she could hope to get rid of us with nothing more than a spray, and least of all somebody as big as the Muffin Man.

Dr. Adams came by this morning to check on everybody's progress. He said I could start going out tomorrow as long as I didn't go swimming, which is perfectly all right with me since the main problem is just to get outside again. It is a lot harder than Squid thinks to keep watch on the Spy Lady from inside Hamsterdam. In fact, it is worse than hard. I haven't told him this yet as I don't think he feels good enough to hear it, but the truth is I haven't even been able to as much as spot the Spy Lady drifting past her windows for more than a day now!?! But as there is nothing I can do about the situation, alas, until the morrow, I shall now get on with my plan for solving the Mad Sophie portion of the Spy Lady Case, and maybe more.

I must start by explaining that it is not completely original as I got it from William Shakespeare when I was sick and Father was reading aloud to me and the others. The play that gave me the idea was *The Tragedy of Hamlet, Prince of Denmark* when he, Hamlet, gets the Players to act out the murder of his father the King in order to startle his mother the Queen and his uncle the Villain into a Confession. My stratagem, then, is for the S.S.F.T.D.A.S.O.C. to do exactly the same thing, to wit: present a play that will enact the murder of Mad Sophie and so will have this same startling effect on the Spy Lady.

162

I am interrupted by a bolt of lightning which has just struck. Not actually, of course, although it might as well have been for all the confusion it has wrought!

I heard the kitchen door slam as Oma came rushing back in from the Vegetable Man's truck out in front.

"I just saw Dr. Adams!" she cried, as though this could possibly be news.

"He's here again?"

"Not here," said Oma. "There!"

"Where's there?" I asked, not even looking up from the Log, and that is when the lightning struck.

"Next door with Madame Symond, and what do you think?" Oma said, overcome by her own news. "Now *she* has got the mumps!"

My first thought was dismay as this would naturally delay the opening of our play and ergo the solution to Mad Sophie. But then the full realization of what Oma said hit me, and I ran to tell the others who likewise staggered under the blow of this new mystery. For as the Arab pointed out, even if we had built a tunnel from our house to next door and set the mump germs in it, they still couldn't have found their way to her, *so how then did the Spy Lady catch our mumps?*

The Mystery of the
Spy Lady Is Solved and
Also a Few Others

———————————

OMELETTE

by Persis Samuel

"That's what you've been writing all this time?" Squid asked incredulously over my shoulder.

"It's a pretty short menu if you ask me," said the Arab.

"Can I see?" said the Contessa.

But I am choosing to ignore these comments and hope they will go away as an author must have some peace and quiet to work and also anybody with even a pea's brain could tell that the above is the title of my play, so-called, of course, because of Hamlet.

Only my story then goes on to differ v. much from the original as, for instance, the main character is not a hero prince of Denmark but a heroine spy of France, to wit: Omelette.

"To wit To wit To wit," Squid tweeted, still perched at my shoulder. "That's all you ever write. Are we keeping a Log Book or a bunch of bird calls?"

Father says we must be patient with Hamilton as his was the worst case of mumps, and it is pretty hard to be the last one sick and have to lie around convalescing when everybody else is up, esp. when you are used to being so active. Which is much truer than Fthr. even knows, although you'd think as the Spy Lady herself is down with mumps and safely in quarantine, Squid wouldn't be so worried about business.

He says, though, you can't trust a sick spy any more than a healthy one and maybe less as they're apt to be more desperate. In fact, as soon as he heard the news about the Spy Lady's mumps, he sneaked his old periscope into bed so he could keep a personal eye on her house. Which is how he happened to see the florist deliver that enormous bouquet. There were so many flowers Squid nearly popped a mump blowing his bos'n's whistle for us as he was afraid it was

167

some kind of funeral wreath. It wasn't, of course, but then we had another thought almost as bad, to wit: who would be sending the Spy Lady flowers except the Muffin Man? And how could they be from him unless he is still lurking somewhere around!?!

Shortly after this the periscope got confiscated by Fthr. as it was made out of quite a large piece of drainpipe and v. hard to conceal under the covers.

"I thought this was supposed to be your precious *Omelette?*" Squid said, back and grumbling over my shoulder again. "Looks more like scrambled brains to me."

Dr. Adams told Fthr. that Hamilton will be himself in a few more days, and as that means the worst is still to come, I had better hurry on with my work.

At first I was planning to copy out the whole (III Acts, XIV Scenes) of "Omelette," but as there is not much room left in the Log Book, I have decided just to sum up the plot enough to show how we mean to trap the Spy Lady.

A Summary of OMELETTE

Omelette is paid an unexpected visit by the mysterious Sophelia whom she has not seen for a while, although in their younger days they used to spy together all the time.

When Sophelia with a sinister laugh lets out that she knows about how Omelette got rather slaughtered over her last piece of work, Omelette realizes that it must have been none other than Sophelia herself who had been behind the conspiracy. She also realizes that she will have to get rid of Sophelia before it's the other way around again.

So one sunny day she slips her a good stiff draft of poison at lunch time, after which Sophelia slowly collapses in the garden, although in a v. natural-looking way. After dark Omelette hides the body of Sophelia safely away and when

Le Comte de Brioche who is actually the head of the Spy Ring contacts Omelette, she reports the whole incident to him. She speaks of how Sophelia "is gone. But not, unhappily without first a little (throaty chuckle) assistance, *comprenez-vous?*" and how she, Omelette, had "not wanted to hurt her but had to get rid of her" in order "to protect oneself, one's work," and so forth and so on.

Well, when the Spy Lady hears her very own past words coming out of Omelette's mouth like that, she will turn deathly pale and realize that the play is no mere coincidence but that all is known by the S.S.F.T.D.A.S.O.C. and there is no alternative left but to give herself up.

We have been concentrating all efforts on getting *Omelette* ready to present. It is taking a whole lot longer than I thought, and we are beginning to worry that our time is running out as the other day Dr. Adams mentioned to Oma what a light case of mumps the Spy Lady had got and how she was practically up already. We have been working extra hard since this last medical report and have finished fixing up the stage in the boathouse, but still must make the posters to put around the village and print up all the tickets. We're hoping to sell out the whole theater at $0.25 a seat as there can be only one performance and we figure that the S.S.F.T.D.A.S.O.C. might as well make a good profit while we're at it, except, of course, from the Spy Lady who we will naturally have to give a free ticket to so as to make sure she comes.

We have been holding rehearsals in Squid's room after hours although nobody knows his lines yet and keeps dropping off to sleep. Except I, who am playing the part of "Omelette," and so have to keep talking. I think I have got the Spy Lady's accent copied pretty well although the Arab says my voice has got to get deeper and more husky. Squid says brandy will do that, but the Arab said it would take years that way and he will invent me something quicker.

I break off the above entry to report the following urgent telephone call which has just come in from the Arab who went uptown to buy some red poster-board.

Local Telephone Call to Hamsterdam
from the Arab

The Arab: The Arab here.
The Contessa: Jared? Are you calling from a telephone booth? What're you calling for if you have to pay?
The Arab: Listen, this is serious. Put on Eustacia.
Eustacia: Eustacia here.
The Arab: This is the Arab. I need help. Meet me behind Moby Dick.
Eustacia: What's up, Arab?
The Arab: The Spy Lady is! And that's not all. The Muffin Man's back again!
Eustacia: I'm putting on my wig. We'll be right there.

We have returned. I can hardly bring myself to write what has taken place but must get the report down quickly as our Special Crisis Meeting is scheduled to begin in a very few minutes. The S.S.F.T.D.A.S.O.C. has just suffered a most terrible blow, and it seems as though all the work on poor *Omelette,* among other things, has been but for naught. I know a writer should be able to tell the facts, even when they are awful, without her feelings mixed in, and I will try, but it certainly isn't easy.

The Contessa and I joined the Arab behind the Moby Dick statue as arranged. From here we observed the Spy Lady and the Muffin Man sitting at the Bonsoir Cafe, looking just exactly like before, including even the usual paper bag of blueberry muffins. They stayed talking over what the Arab said was already their second cups of coffee for a while longer and then got up and crossed over to the Wharf, with the Arab and the Contessa and I close behind. Even though they were walking at a good pace, they kept on talking with their heads close together all the way out on the Wharf, although I suppose this was not surprising as they must have had a lot of espionage business to catch up on since last they met.

At about this time the Boston steamer was docking and blowing its horn like anything. There was a big crowd of confusion milling around, and as the Contessa and I were concentrating v. hard on keeping up with the Spy Lady and the Muffin Man, we did not notice who was coming down off the steamer gangway until we heard the Arab give a loud, startled cry as though he had just seen a ghost, and no wonder.

"It's Mad Sophie!!!" he gasped.

Special Crisis Meeting of the
S.S.F.T.D.A.S.O.C.

President: I'm going to get right to the point. This Special Crisis meeting has been called because three agents of this outfit have turned up with the weird report that they witnessed the arrival of the deceased Madeleine Sophie Lehman-Chottley on the 1600 steamer from Boston and with their very own eyes saw her actually walk off down the street.

The Arab: We never said street, we said wharf.

Squid: Shut up, can't you? This is a matter of life and death, for God's sake. (pause) Do the three of you solemnly insist and swear that this incredible sight was made up of real blood and bones and was in no way merely a transmitted apparition from outer space or some kind of earthly ghost?

The Arab:
Eustacia: } We do so solemnly swear.
The Contessa:

Squid: I don't believe it. (sigh) Let's run through the facts again, nice and slow. The Arab starts.

The Arab: Just what I already told you a hundred times, Squid. I happen to look up when the steamer's docked, and the first thing I see coming down the gangplank is Mad Sophie.

The Contessa: She was wearing the same coat and gold earrings and everything.

Eustacia: And she was with this friend, talking away just like before, as though she didn't have a care in the world, let alone had been murdered.

Squid: OK. Go on. Then what happened?

The Arab: We already told you. Nothing. She gets off the boat and walks right past the Spy Lady with her nose stuck up in the air like she hardly knows her.

The Contessa: She looked back twice over her shoulder, though, to see the Muffin Man.

Eustacia: Well, that is perfectly understandable. I mean we have grown accustomed to the way he looks, but you have to remember he is still a pretty sinister sight if you are just seeing him for the first time.

Squid: So then?

The Arab: Then we ran home to tell you.

Squid: I still don't believe it. Mad Sophie up and walking around in her own missing body! It's a pretty messy business if you ask me. Do any of you care to venture an explanation of this strange state of affairs?

The Contessa: The Spy Lady never murdered her!

The Arab: She must have just fallen asleep that day on the beach.

The Contessa: Because she always stayed up so late at night talking.

Squid: Wait a minute. Just hold it a minute. I think I'm beginning to piece the whole thing together, and I'm not so sure Mad Sophie even fits. I mean maybe she is not only not dead, she might not even be a real part of this plot.

The Arab: Or counterplot. Especially if she didn't even recognize the Muffin Man.

Eustacia: That's what I'm beginning to think. Only she kept talking so much the Spy Lady couldn't concentrate on her work—

The Arab: So she finally told her she had to go home. And that's how she got rid of her.

Squid: It certainly explains why we never found the body. Still, if it comes down to that, I guess I'd almost rather the Spy Lady didn't commit a murder than that we were too dumb to solve it. (pause) So I guess this hereby clears the Spy Lady of any real homicidal intent.

The Contessa: Hooray!

Squid: Order!

May I remind the S.S.F.T.D.A.S.O.C. that although the Spy Lady's no longer under suspicion of murder— for the moment—there's still a little matter of espionage to clear up. I mean there are still two foreign agents at large, of which she is one, don't forget.

The Arab: Hear! Hear!

Squid: And hear this: We have got to break this case before it breaks us. I am now going to make a special motion that we four vow on our own sacred blood that from this moment forward we will bend all efforts and will to one end only: The final solution of the Spy Lady and the Muffin Man.

The Arab: And the collection of the Reward.

Eustacia: I second the motion.
President: All in favor say aye.
All: Aye!

It is only three days later, and yet I am writing in the Log Book for what may be the last time as the Case of the Spy Lady has been solved and her file will soon be closed, although never I think forgotten.

Between the other day's meeting and today's end of the Case, there occurred only a few more incidents, but these were enough. I am going to put them down now in a slow and careful hand to see if written out like that, large and black, this unexpected and, indeed, astonishing, turn of events will be any easier for us to believe.

The morning after the Special Crisis meeting, Squid got disguised along with the rest of us, and we smuggled him across the roof and down over the side of the top deck as he was not yet allowed out of the house because of still recuperating.

The Spy Lady was not anywhere at home but the Bentley was, and determined to hunt down every possible clue, we went over all car door handles for fingerprints and also inspected the tires as Squid said you never know what they can pick up.

After this we hurried along Bay Street into the village, and here luck was with us as almost at once the Contessa spotted the Spy Lady, despite her being well covered by a large and floppy straw hat. She was coming out of the Town Library and was followed a step or two behind by the Muffin Man.

"What're they after in there?" said the Arab.

"It's a good quiet place to talk," Squid said.

We quickly split up, the Arab darting behind the path's long hedge while the Contessa, Squid, and I stayed in back of a big clump of bushes. The Spy Lady and the Muffin Man came down the walk, moving very slowly and carefully. They did not speak at all but kept suspiciously glancing around, esp. at the hedge, and, horrified, we three finally saw why. For although the Arab was well hidden, his black homburg was not and, in fact, could clearly be seen several inches above the hedge as it moved along, following the Spy Lady and the Muffin Man at a discreet distance.

There was no way, alas, to signal the Arab, and in any case it was too late, for the Muffin Man, suspecting that there was probably more than just a hat on their tail, wrote out a quick message, passed it to the Spy Lady, and fled. She hurried away in the opp. direction but a little way up the street stopped to read it, after which, with a furtive look around, she folded the note twice over and tore it in four. Squid got all set to spring up after the pieces, but he never got the chance as instead of throwing them away, she calmly popped them into her mouth and, to our amazement, chewed the whole thing up!?!

Squid swore all the way back home and, to tell the truth, so did the rest of us as it was pretty frustrating to have to watch a top-secret document walk off that way. Still, as the Arab said, you almost had to admire the Spy Lady as not everybody would have thought of eating up the evidence so quickly.

The next morning we were back on the Case at about 0930, which was not nearly as early as scheduled. This was due to our having been up so late the night before with Father who took us out for lobster rolls and then to the Art Cinema to celebrate being practically finished with his sculpture. He is as mysterious as usual about what it is, if not more so, and says we shall see for ourselves when it is time. Whatever it is, though, it must be turning out even better than he had hoped as we have hardly ever seen him so cheerful with a job. And I just wish I could say the same for ours.

Late as we were getting to work, the Spy Lady and the Muffin Man were even later, and it was almost noon before we picked up their trail going into the Bonsoir Cafe. This time we were ready for them. While we others hid behind the trellis border, the Arab followed them to a nearby table with a copy of the *Scrimshaw Weekly* newspaper. He propped it up wide open in front of him not unlike Fthr. at breakfast, except far from reading the news the Arab was watching it through some clever little eye slits he had made in the newspaper. The main object of the mission, though, was to listen, and it looked like the Arab had achieved his goal, for he was close enough to hear every word that passed between the Muffin Man and the Spy Lady. Only to our consternation none ever did as the Muffin Man got up almost at once, not even staying long enough to give an order to the waiter, much less the Spy Lady.

"I thought you said this was foolproof," I whispered to Squid.

"I guess I underestimated our fool," Squid replied bitterly, and then I saw that the Arab was sitting there pretending to read a paper, which in his excitement he was holding upside down! Yet something more shattering was still in store. As the Muffin Man followed by the Spy Lady passed the Arab's table, he paused just long enough to casually lift the newspaper from the Arab's dumbstruck hands and turn it right side up for him!?!

This shook us to our very roots and also filled us with a terrible uncertainty as we had no way of knowing whether this had been simply a kindly neighborly gesture, as the Contessa suggested, or whether, as the rest of us strongly suspected, it had been a subtle but sinister warning from one undercover agent who knew he was being shadowed to another.

"It's just a lucky thing it's such a busy cafe. I mean there's no telling what kind of close call the Arab here just missed," Squid said, giving him a much kindlier look.

"Maybe the Spy Lady and him's on to our whole organization," the Arab said, his face showing very white where his mask ended.

"So we'll just have to speed things up, that's all. Only no more solitary missions—it's way too dangerous. From now on we all work together, even Parvis." Squid stroked his beard thoughtfully. "I've got a strange feeling we're coming to some kind of showdown," he added, and as it happened, he was quite right. Especially about the some kind part.

The first crack and the subsequent break in the Case came even sooner than we had dared to hope, and for this all praise and tribute must go straight to Parvis. For once again, just like with last summer's Smugglers, the day was saved by his infallible instinct, speed, and fortitude, and this time he wasn't even drunk.

What happened was this: On the following morn. from 0830 to 1030 the Spy Lady worked over her notebook on the sun deck. From 1030 to 1100 she played her violin in the living room. At 1130 she left the house in a silky white kaftan sort of dress with a hood which she put up (!) and dark glasses, and proceeded at a brisk pace up to the village, Squid, the Arab, Parvis, me, and the Contessa stealthily shadowing her, in that order. We arriv. at the main wharf a little before the noon blast, and here is where the excitement, and Parvis, broke loose. Whereas the rest of us were totally absorbed in following the Spy Lady out on the tourist-crowded wharf, where we later realized she must have planned to give us the slip, Parvis stopped cold, gave a long quivering sniff, and bolted back down the wharf and over to Greta's Coffee Shop. A moment later we saw why. There next to the doorway, clutching his bakery bag in his big black gloves, lurked the Muffin Man, as dim as the shadow

177

he stood in. His coat collar pulled high nearly covered his huge whiskers, and his cap came low over his dark glasses. The moment he saw Parvis coming at him, he tried to back up into Fat Greta's but couldn't because a pair of tourists were coming out, and so instead he bolted for it. In his confusion and haste he dropped the paper bag full of blueberry muffins, and, far more important, a folded note. Parvis went after the muffins while the rest of us quickly encircled the note, which had obviously been meant for the Spy Lady. Squid, pale with excitement, carefully picked it up by the edge and opened it to reveal, as we suspected it would, the following enciphered message.

1355201351202085

19202149151206152118

"I don't get it," said the Contessa.

"Of course you don't. That's why it's a code, you nut."

The Arab shook his head doubtfully. "It's going to take more than a sledgehammer to break this one, Squid."

"All the more reason to hurry then. Besides," Squid said, mopping his brow, "I've got a hunch we're really running out of time."

The fact is we were all beginning to have that same nervous feeling, and hurriedly wrapping up the note in the Arab's red bandanna, we raced back home and settled down to work in Squid's room. It was by now nearly 1300, and we started off by going over the note for fingerprints but found none at all.

"Well, naturally," I said. "How could there be when he's always wearing those horrible old gloves?"

"Elementary, my dear Eustacia. If you'd have ever taken a good look at those gloves, you'd have seen they were made, in fact, out of special leather like those ones Father got in Italy, with a lot of good tough wrinkles that would have to show up, like a rhinoceros hide."

"A rhinoceros!" the Contessa began to protest, but the Arab quickly interrupted her, saying if that was the case, then either the fingerprint powder had gone stale or the message was actually written on some kind of extra-terrestrial substance which only looked like paper. He and Squid then gave the note a paper test (fire and water), which it passed 100%.

It was now almost 1330, and getting out the cipher clock, letter frequency chart, etc., we began what soon appeared to be the impossible task of breaking down the code. We tried everything we knew from the Double Parallel-Alphabet to Lord Wolseley's Square, but nothing would give way.

Squid rubbed at his eyes and sighed. "There's only one more thing I can think of: that's the old Greek alphabet square figure cipher."

The Contessa looked up from counting on her fingers. "I think it's a lot simpler than that," she said. "I bet it's just plain A equals 1."

Which of course is exactly what it turned out to do and, as Squid said, had we not been led astray by the Muffin Man's diabolically clever simplicity, we'd have seen through the code at once. As it was, however, it was 1520 before the note was deciphered into the following alarming message.

mee t	me	a t	t he
135520	135	120	2085

s t u di o	a t	f o u r
1920214915	120	6152118

"Studio!?" said the Arab.

"Whose studio, Ham?" the Contessa asked in a small, trembling voice, for although Scrimshaw is as full of studios as it is artists, I think from that first moment we all knew with a terrible dread certainty that it was going to be Father's. We looked at each other in horror, remembering the times the Spy Lady and the Muffin Man had been spotted around there, and like the others, I felt myself grow pale with fear over the danger poor Fthr. was in.

Squid was the first to recover. "What time is it?" he said, jumping to his feet.

"Exactly 1522."

"Good. With luck we'll get there before they do." He whistled for Parvis, and the five of us took off to warn Father, racing up Bay Street as fast as we could. In fact, I don't think we ever ran so fast in our whole lives, and all the while our hearts were jumping around inside like a bunch of crazy lunatics. What the Spy Lady and the Muffin Man could want with Fthr. and/or the Studio, I must admit was a mystery to me, but as Squid pointed out, that's what the whole thing was.

The Arab and the Contessa started yelling out to Father the minute we got in the downstairs door, but there was no answer. The only sound we could hear in the heavy afternoon silence was our own scared breathing, and we knew even before we got all the way upstairs to the Studio that it was going to be empty.

We rushed into the loft and then stopped, even Parvis, and stood there for a moment caught in the awful stillness. There was sunshine coming in the windows and down the skylight, and yet the way Father's sculptures stood around so deathly still, some draped, others not, and the way everything, even the sunlight was covered with clay dust, for an awful moment we felt as though we had come barging into King Tut's Tomb.

The Arab cleared his throat. "I guess Father's not here," he whispered.

"It's probably best that way," Squid replied, rubbing his hands together and, you could see, sounding a lot more brisk than he felt. "He's well out of it."

He walked out to the middle of the studio and turned around thoughtfully. "OK, here's the plan. We'll spread a net for them. What we'll do is: we'll go into hiding now, each of us in a different corner of the room, see, and by the time the Muffin Man and the Spy Lady show up, they'll be completely surrounded."

Squid started to assign the cover positions, circling quickly around the studio. He was getting excited as was Parvis, who now began yipping at his heels.

"The Arab goes behind that screen over there," Squid said. "Down, boy, quiet!" This last remark was directed at Parvis, of course, not the Arab, although it might as well have been, for as he reached his post behind the screen, he let out a horrible little yip himself.

"What is it?" Squid called as we rushed to his side.

"It's the Spy Lady's head," the Arab gasped, as indeed we now saw for ourselves it was. She, it, sat in the middle of Fthr's high workbench. A thin layer of damp cheesecloth covered the molded clay features, but there wasn't a doubt in the world that they were the Spy Lady's, which I believe by now we could have recognized had they been covered by a paper bag.

"What's she doing here!?!" Squid muttered, but while we were still staggering from this shock, Parvis suddenly appeared from Fthr's little dressing room with another. Growling happily, he slid and slipped across the floor, half dragging and half wrestling with a long brown muffler.

"It's the Muffin Man's!" Squid cried, and surprised out of his usual caution, he ran directly into the dressing room. Not an instant later he was back in the doorway, his eyes popping straight out of his head.

"The Muffin Man's in there," he said, in a strange, strangled voice. "He's hanging up in there."

The Contessa gave a shrill little cry, and I felt the color draining away even from my mask. Slowly we followed the Arab into the dressing room, the Contessa clutching me with one hand and covering up her eyes with the other. And

I must admit that what we saw was more than enough to cry about.

The Muffin Man was hanging there all right, but on one of Father's wooden hangers!

The Arab's mouth fell open. "I don't believe it!" he gasped.

Nor could we others, and yet there the Muffin Man was, or at least most of him: the trench coat with tremendous padded shoulders, the dark brown trousers, the cap, the rhinoceros gloves, and, parked below, the black shoes.

"The rest of him's over there," Squid said, nodding grimly toward Fthr's dressing table. We walked slowly over to it, and there, sure enough, were the big handlebar moustaches, the old-fashioned mutton-chop whiskers, the Dutchman's beard, all neatly laid out, with the great hawk nose and dark glasses sitting in the middle.

The Arab shook his head. "I don't get it," he said.

"Don't you?" replied Squid.

We Come to
an Unexpected End

Not that Squid had got everything figured out right away either, for in those first baffling moments we none of us knew what to think. Except, that is, for the Contessa.

"How'd his stuff get here?" said the Arab.

"It's simple," she cried, a joyous grin stretching far beyond her wax lips. "It's Father who's the Muffin Man! He got disguised to keep it a secret he was sculpturing the Spy Lady! So it would be a surprise!"

If I have ever before said there was a stunned silence, it could only have been pretty noisy compared to this one.

"What?" the Arab finally said, sitting down v. weakly.

"Oh, no," Squid moaned, his face, like this old Log page, white in the middle and yellowing at the edges.

Well, it was certainly a surprise all right, nor could it be denied, for once the Contessa had spoken, things began to fall into place like a fast trick shuffle of cards.

"I thought there was something familiar about him," the Arab said.

"All those blueberry muffins!" I remembered ruefully.

"And the rhinoceros gloves!" Squid groaned.

By the time we had reached home we had got pretty much the whole thing figured out. In fact, the big mystery now was how come we hadn't solved it any sooner? Although if it hadn't been Fthr., I'm sure we would have, for despite how Squid has always said you can't trust anyone in this business, who'd have thought of suspecting their very own father?!?

He and the Spy Lady were home waiting for us, naturally, Father grinning exactly like the Contessa, and the pieces of the plot we couldn't put together, they did. Such as how Fthr. had been commissioned by the Spy Lady's publishers to do her head, which they may even use on the jacket of her new book as it turns out the closest she has ever come to espionage is writing about it!

"So that's what's in the notebooks," Squid said. "I might have known!"

And as the Contessa guessed, once Father saw we were hot on the trail of the Spy Lady, somewhat mistakenly, I admit, he realized he'd have to go undercover too, just like us, if he wanted to get his work done in any peace. Which is pretty flattering when you come to think about it. I mean Fthr. taking a page from our book like that, so to speak.

"I guess two can play at this game," he said, not without a certain pride.

The Spy Lady shyly gave her sunburst smile. "Seven," she murmured in her low voice, counting, of course, Parvis, who was sitting in her lap, or as much as he could considering that the Contessa had got there first.

The others said in order to keep the Log record straight it ought to be pointed out that we did hit pretty close to the mark on some of the targets. For instance, the Spy Lady told us we'd got it figured out exactly right about Mad Sophie. All but the murder, that is. She thought it was v. funny that we thought she had got nearly slaughtered by counteragents when what they were actually were literary critics.

"I should have minded much less the agents, I think," she laughed. In fact, once everybody got to talking, the whole thing began to strike us members of the S.S.F.T.D.A.S.O.C. as kind of funny, even Squid.

To tell the truth, after that eve. we did not even regret the loss of a Spy Lady so much as at first, I must admit, the loss of the Reward. The Spy Lady, I mean Therese, for that is what the T. stands for, hearing about the empty condition of the Mutual Fund from the Treasurer who can be an awful little blabbermouth once the fake teeth are out, generously offered a Reward anyway as she said we did in a way solve the Case of the Spy Lady. We politely refused it, of course, although it wasn't easy, especially as it seems she could well

186

afford to pay a price on her own head, due to a recent legacy from her Great-Aunt who, as it turns out, is the only person in this Log Book, I guess, who really is dead. And despite Squid gave the Spy Lady a strange, shrewd look upon hearing this information, I am certain it was of natural causes.

I see now with a sad feeling that there's only a few blank pages left in the Log Book, and I shall probably have come to the end of them before it's time to go over to ~~the Spy Lady's~~, Therese's house. She is helping us to get ready to put on *Omelette,* for as Squid said, even if it didn't trap her, it might accidentally catch somebody else and meanwhile, as the Arab pointed out, the admission money will help keep the Mutual Fund going till the next job comes along.

We were over at the Spy Lady's yesterday, too, and she gave us tea with cakes. She even had out a dish of raw fish for Icarus, at least we think it was for him. It was all v. delicious, too, especially as now we don't have to worry about whether anything's been poisoned or not. And last night the Spy Lady came to dinner here. It was quite a festive occasion. The Contessa set the table with her fish napkin rings, we others gathered a big bouquet of sea lavender, and Oma got so excited she made two different kinds of apple strudel.

In fact, I guess we have been seeing the Spy Lady almost as much as before, although a lot closer to, of course. For what Fthr. didn't exactly say, although you don't have to be a secret agent to have figured it out, is that I guess like Pygmalion he began to get v. fond of the statue he was working on. Not that we blame him, either, for to tell the truth, so have we. Even Squid.

"I guess she's not so bad even if she isn't a Spy Lady," he said the other night.

Oma just came in to light the fire, for though the sun is

187

still bright, the air has gone quite cold, and now we are all sitting around the fireplace, even Parvis and James and Icarus.

Rachel is on the floor playing on her flute. She is trying to get her moon snail to come out of his shell, but he isn't of course, which is pretty understandable when you consider how off-key she is.

Ham is oiling and polishing up a whole bunch of telescopes, field glasses, calipers, and so forth.

"Why don't you come help me with some of this equipment?" he has just grunted at Jared."What're you doing over there anyway?"

Jared went on turning the pages of the big old Capt's book he held in his lap. "Trying to find a recipe to make whale perfume."

Rachel gave a surprised and happy squeal. "Whale perfume!" she cried. "Why, Jared Samuel, that's the nicest, kindest idea I ever heard of!"

Jared snorted. *"From* whales, you idiot," he said. "Not for."

I have nearly finished the last page of the Log Book. Beside me the fire crackles and spits out bits of burned wood. I look out the window over the bay, and a gull cries as it goes coasting sideways on a brisk chill wind. I can see now that the summer has come to an end, and so I think have we.